The Purr-fect Cover-Up

When the Truth Has Nine Lives

Marina Clearwater

Copyright © 2024 by Marina Clearwater

All rights reserved. No part of this book may be used or reproduced in any form whatsoever without written permission except in the case of brief quotations in critical articles or reviews.

First Edition: December 2024

Table of Contents

Chapter 1
The Feline Intrigue

The rain lashed against the cracked window of Rex Barkley's office, drumming an uneven rhythm that matched the tapping of his claws against his battered desk. The dim glow of a flickering desk lamp cast long, jagged shadows across the room, illuminating piles of unsorted papers and a coffee mug that had seen more whiskey than caffeine. The hound slouched in his chair, his trench coat rumpled like a worn flag of surrender. Barkington City had a way of grinding you down until you either crawled or quit.

Rex leaned back, his chair creaking under his weight, and sighed. Business had been drier than his sense of humor, and his rent wasn't going to pay itself. He reached for the jar on his desk labeled "Bacon Fund" and shook it. The pitiful clink of a lone coin rattling around inside was the answer to his unspoken question. It might be time to pack it in, maybe find a less hazardous way to make a living. He'd had enough scars to last a lifetime, and for what? Cases that never quite covered the bills.

As he considered the grim prospect of closing shop, a faint scent wafted through the cracks of the door—a curious mix of jasmine and danger. His ears perked, his nose twitching at the subtle promise of trouble. Moments later, a soft but deliberate knock echoed through the room, cutting through the rhythm of the rain.

"Come in," Rex called, his voice gravelly but steady. He straightened in his chair, his eyes narrowing as the frosted glass door swung open.

She stepped in, her silhouette sharp against the neon haze of the city outside. A Siamese, sleek and elegant, with a diamond-studded collar that sparkled like a taunt in the dim light. Her coat was pristine, a testament to either wealth or vanity—or both. The click of her claws on the floor was deliberate, like a metronome set to slow jazz. She didn't walk; she owned the space she moved through.

"Detective Barkley," she said, her voice smooth as silk with just the faintest edge of a purr. "I hope I'm not interrupting."

"That depends," Rex replied, leaning forward. His eyes flicked to her collar, then back to her icy blue gaze. "You bringing trouble, or just passing through?"

"Trouble?" She smiled faintly, her lips curling in a way that suggested she enjoyed the word. "No, Detective. I'm here to solve it."

Rex gestured to the chair across from his desk, the only one not buried under clutter. It wobbled slightly as she sat, but she maintained her poise, her tail curling elegantly around her paws. He could feel the weight of her gaze as she sized him up, as if she were the one deciding whether he was worth her time.

"So, what brings a classy dame like you to my humble little corner of the city?" Rex asked, pulling a notepad from the clutter. His tone was casual, but his instincts were on high alert.

She let the silence linger for just a moment too long, her claws tracing an idle pattern on the edge of his desk. "A theft," she said finally. "Something of great value has been stolen from me. I need it recovered discreetly."

Rex raised an eyebrow. "Discreet, huh? You don't strike me as the discreet type."

Her smile didn't falter, but her eyes sharpened. "Appearances can be deceiving, Detective."

"I'll bet," Rex muttered, jotting down the word "theft" on his pad. "What was taken?"

"A family heirloom," she said, her voice softening just slightly, as if the words were difficult to form. "A diamond-encrusted bone. It's... priceless. Both in sentimental and financial value."

Rex's pencil paused mid-scratch. "A diamond-encrusted bone? Fancy chewables you've got in the family."

"It's more than a chewable," she replied, her tone tightening ever so slightly. "It's a symbol of loyalty, of legacy. And now it's gone."

Rex leaned back, studying her carefully. Her story was polished, too polished. Every word felt rehearsed, like a melody played so often it had lost its original rhythm. "Who took it?"

"I suspect the Alley Cartel," she said, the name slipping off her tongue like a hiss. "They've been circling my family for years, waiting for a moment of weakness. Last night, they found one."

"And you want me to get it back," Rex said, his voice flat. "That's a tall order for a guy working out of a secondhand office with a bacon jar for a retirement fund."

She tilted her head, her expression a mix of amusement and challenge. "I hear you solve problems, Detective. This one should be no different."

Rex tapped his pencil against the desk, his eyes narrowing. The scent of jasmine mingled with something darker now, something he couldn't quite place. "What's the catch?"

"No catch," she said, her smile returning. "Just results."

Rex didn't believe her. Not entirely. But the promise of payment was too good to ignore, and the fire in her gaze suggested walking away wasn't an option. He closed his notebook with a snap and stood, pulling his trench coat from the back of his chair.

"Alright, Miss..." He let the word hang in the air.

"Whiskers," she said smoothly, rising to her feet. "Miss Whiskers."

Rex adjusted his hat, the rain tapping against the window like an impatient drumbeat. "Alright, Miss Whiskers. You've got yourself a detective."

Her smile deepened, just enough to reveal the satisfaction beneath her polished exterior. "I knew I could count on you, Detective Barkley."

As she turned to leave, her silhouette lingered in the doorway, framed by the faint glow of neon. Rex watched her go, his instincts barking at him to stay clear, but his wallet growling louder.

"Trouble," he muttered under his breath. "Always looks good in diamonds."

The rain had eased to a murmur by the time Rex stepped into the penthouse. The quiet hum of the elevator ride up had given him time to wonder why a cat like Miss Whiskers, dripping in diamonds and entitlement, needed a gumshoe like him. He figured it wasn't for his sparkling personality. She led him through the open double doors, the scent of lavender clinging to the air.

The penthouse was as polished as its owner: sleek, spotless marble floors, art pieces that screamed "don't touch," and furniture so pristine it seemed allergic to imperfection. Except for the mess by the shattered window. Glass fragments littered the floor, catching the faint light like jagged stars.

"Let me guess," Rex said, his voice cutting through the tension like a dull blade. "You don't have a cleaning service, or they didn't cover staged burglaries?"

Miss Whiskers cast him a sharp glance but didn't bite. Instead, she gestured toward the window with one manicured paw. "They came in last night, broke through that window," she began, her tone as measured as her steps. "Ransacked the place. But as you can see, they weren't looking for just anything. They knew exactly what they wanted."

"Your bone," Rex said flatly, crouching to examine the floor. His nose twitched at the faint scent of catnip mixed with... something fishy. "Diamond-encrusted, sentimental, and all that."

"Yes," she replied, her tail swishing. "But it's not just an heirloom. It's a legacy. My great-grandfather, Lord Whiskerly, had it commissioned. It represents the Whiskers name, Detective. And now, it's gone."

Rex picked up a shard of glass, rolling it between his fingers. "Funny thing about this window," he muttered. "Glass is scattered inside. If they broke in, wouldn't more of it end up outside?"

She didn't flinch. "I noticed that too. It's why I believe this wasn't just some petty thief. It was planned."

"Planned, huh?" Rex straightened, his eyes narrowing. "That's a big leap for someone who called me an hour ago claiming it was the Alley Cartel."

Miss Whiskers gave a delicate shrug, her diamond collar catching the light. "They've been after my family's possessions for years. Who else could it be?"

Rex walked the perimeter of the scene, boots crunching on stray shards. His gaze landed on faint muddy pawprints trailing toward the shattered window, too perfect to be accidental. "Muddy prints indoors," he said, scratching his chin. "You keep an indoor garden I don't know about?"

"Hardly," she said, her tone tight. "Detective, do you always question your clients with this level of suspicion, or am I special?"

"You're special," Rex replied without missing a beat. He bent closer to the pawprints, sniffing. "Too special for these prints to look this clean. If I didn't know better, I'd say someone wanted me to see them."

Her tail flicked, betraying the first crack in her composure. "What are you implying, Detective?"

"I'm not implying anything," he said, standing. "Not yet, anyway. But whoever did this went through a lot of trouble to make it look messy without actually being messy. They even left a calling card."

He pointed toward a faint glyph etched into the marble floor near the window. It was subtle but deliberate, the kind of mark that didn't get there by accident. Miss Whiskers' gaze followed his gesture, her expression unreadable.

"Do you recognize it?" Rex asked, watching her closely.

Her pause was almost imperceptible, but Rex caught it. "No," she said finally, her voice smooth. "Should I?"

"Maybe," he said, not buying it. "Looks like someone wanted to send a message. Trouble is, I don't know if it's for you or for me."

She turned toward him, her icy blue eyes locking onto his. "That's why I hired you, Detective. To figure it out."

Rex crossed his arms, his skepticism warring with the weight of his empty bacon jar back at the office. "You've got means," he said. "Plenty of them, by the looks of this place. Why not hire someone with more... polish?"

"Polish doesn't solve problems," she said, her voice cool but firm. "You do."

Rex let out a short laugh, shaking his head. "Flattery's nice, but it doesn't pay the rent. What's in it for me?"

She stepped closer, her tail swishing softly against the air. "Ten thousand kibble," she said, the words rolling off her tongue like an offer too good to refuse. "Half now, half when you recover the bone."

Rex arched an eyebrow. "That's a lot of kibble for a chew toy."

"As I said, Detective," she replied, her tone cutting, "it's not just a chew toy."

The rain tapped faintly against the glass, filling the silence that followed. Rex looked back at the glyph, the pawprints, the shattered window. His gut told him this was trouble wrapped in silk and diamonds, but his wallet didn't care.

"Alright, Miss Whiskers," he said finally, pulling his notebook from his pocket. "You've got yourself a detective. But if I find out you're leaving pawprints where they don't belong, we're going to have a different kind of conversation."

She smiled, a slow, satisfied curl of her lips. "I wouldn't dream of it, Detective."

Rex didn't believe her for a second. As he scribbled a few notes and turned toward the door, he couldn't shake the feeling that he'd just stepped into a trap—and she was holding the leash.

Rex stayed behind after Miss Whiskers had excused herself, claiming she had business to attend to in another part of the penthouse. He didn't argue—her absence gave him the breathing room he needed to make sense of the scene without her calculating gaze tracking his every move. The air felt heavy with her perfume, the lavender almost masking the subtler smells beneath it. Almost.

The rain outside had quieted to a gentle drizzle, the city lights casting faint reflections across the polished marble floor. Rex crouched near the broken window, his paw running along the jagged edge of the shattered glass. The shards that lay scattered on the inside caught the faint light like tiny, malevolent stars. He tilted his head, tracing the direction of the fragments with his eyes.

"Funny thing about broken windows," he muttered to himself. "When someone smashes their way in, most of the glass lands outside."

He reached down, picking up a larger shard and holding it to the light. The edge was too clean, too deliberate. Whoever had broken the window hadn't done it in a hurry. This wasn't the work of some thug bashing their way into a penthouse; it was precise, almost practiced. He placed the shard back among its siblings and let his gaze wander toward the muddy pawprints leading away from the window.

Rex followed the trail, his boots making soft scuffs against the marble. The prints were strikingly clear—too clear, in fact. The mud hadn't smudged or smeared as it should have on a surface like this. It was as if someone had pressed them into the floor intentionally. He crouched again, this time near the largest print, and sniffed.

The scent was faint but unmistakable: damp earth with a subtle undertone of something metallic. His nose twitched as he inhaled again, trying to dissect the layers. There it was—fish oil, just the barest trace of it, lingering like a whisper beneath the stronger smells.

Rex sat back on his haunches, his mind clicking through the possibilities. Fish oil wasn't the kind of thing you tracked into a high-end penthouse unless you'd been somewhere like the docks, Barkington's most notorious underbelly. The docks were the kind of place where deals happened in shadows and secrets sunk deeper than the tide.

"Why would a thief break in here, leave pawprints as clean as a Sunday confession, and smell like they just came off a trawler?" he murmured.

He stood, dusting off his knees, and turned his attention to the glyph carved into the floor near the window. It was faint, barely noticeable unless you knew where to look. The design was angular, sharp, and deliberate—more than just a scratch. It looked like a symbol, though not one he recognized.

Rex traced the glyph with a claw, feeling the ridges and grooves. It didn't seem like something left behind in a struggle. No, this was a message, but for whom? And why?

"You finding anything useful, Detective?"

Her voice cut through the quiet like a knife through silk. Rex straightened, turning to see Miss Whiskers leaning against the doorway, her expression calm but her eyes sharp. She looked as if she'd been there for a while, watching him.

"Plenty," he replied, his voice measured. "More questions than answers, though."

She stepped closer, her tail swishing behind her like a pendulum. "Care to share?"

"Sure," Rex said, crossing his arms. "Like why the glass is inside, not outside. Or why the mud prints look more like a display than an accident. And then there's this." He gestured to the glyph. "You sure you don't know what it means?"

Miss Whiskers glanced at the symbol, her expression unreadable. "I've never seen it before," she said smoothly. "Should I?"

"Maybe," Rex replied. "If I didn't know better, I'd say whoever did this wasn't trying to steal your bone. They were trying to send a message."

Her ears flicked, but her composure didn't falter. "That's why I called you, Detective. To figure out what the message means."

Rex let her answer hang in the air for a moment, studying her carefully. Her confidence was unshaken, but there was something in the way she avoided meeting his eyes too directly, something in the way her tail flicked a little too deliberately. She was hiding something—he was sure of it. The question was how much.

"Fair enough," he said finally. "I'll start with the docks. Fish oil doesn't end up in a place like this by accident."

She raised an eyebrow. "The docks? You think this has something to do with the Cartel?"

"It's a hunch," Rex replied, grabbing his notebook from his coat pocket. "And I trust my nose."

Miss Whiskers tilted her head, the faintest hint of a smile tugging at her lips. "Do let me know what you find, Detective."

"Oh, you'll be the first to know," Rex said, heading toward the door. "Just remember—if I find out you're playing me, this little partnership of ours is going to get real uncomfortable, real fast."

Her smile deepened, though her eyes remained as cold and calculating as ever. "I wouldn't dream of it."

Rex didn't bother responding. As he stepped out into the hallway, the faint scent of lavender followed him, mingling with the rain-slick air. His instincts were barking at him, louder than ever. This wasn't just a case of stolen goods. Miss Whiskers wasn't just a client. And somewhere, down by the docks, someone knew exactly what was going on.

The trail was faint, but Rex had it now, and he wasn't the kind of hound to let go once he caught a scent.

Chapter 2
Scent of Trouble

The rain had picked up again, turning the streets of Barkington into a glistening web of slick asphalt and glowing reflections. Neon signs buzzed and flickered in the haze, casting distorted colors onto the puddled sidewalks. Rex Barkley pulled his trench coat tighter against the chill, his fedora dripping with the steady patter of the storm. The scent of fish oil still clung to his nose, faint but persistent, a breadcrumb trail that whispered one word: docks.

Rex moved through the city like a shadow, his boots splashing through shallow puddles as he kept his senses on high alert. The rhythm of his steps was steady, purposeful, but his mind churned with the inconsistencies from Miss Whiskers' penthouse. The glass scattered inside, the pristine muddy pawprints, and the glyph carved into the floor—it all felt too neat, too orchestrated. Someone had gone to a lot of trouble to make the scene look chaotic while keeping it carefully under control.

"Fish oil," he muttered to himself, his voice lost to the rain. "Whoever pulled that stunt didn't just break in. They left a scent trail, and I'll bet my last kibble they wanted me to follow it."

His nose twitched as he paused at a street corner, the faint odor pulling him toward an alley that led deeper into the city. He glanced up, the faint glow of a neon fish market sign flickering in the distance. Barkington's docks were notorious—a labyrinth of warehouses, trawlers, and backroom deals where the air always reeked of saltwater and secrets. If the scent was leading him there, it wasn't by accident.

As he turned down the alley, his ears twitched at the faint sound of shuffling footsteps. He stopped, his hand instinctively brushing the edge of his coat where his notebook rested. The footsteps grew louder, uneven, like someone trying too hard to stay quiet.

"You gonna follow me all night, or you planning to introduce yourself?" Rex called, his voice steady but edged with irritation.

The footsteps paused, and for a moment, the only sound was the rain hitting the pavement. Then, from the shadows, a small figure stepped forward—a scrappy Chihuahua with a trench coat far too big for his wiry frame. His oversized ears twitched nervously as he offered Rex a shaky grin.

"Rex, buddy!" the Chihuahua squeaked, his voice cracking under the weight of forced confidence. "Fancy running into you out here. Small city, huh?"

"Sniffles McGruff," Rex said, narrowing his eyes. "What are you doing skulking around in the rain? Don't tell me you've developed a sudden interest in long walks."

"Skulking?" Sniffles let out a nervous laugh, his paws fidgeting with the edges of his coat. "No skulking here, pal. Just, uh, keeping my ears to the ground, you know? The usual."

Rex sighed, pinching the bridge of his nose. "Cut the act, Sniffles. You're sniffing around for a reason. What do you know about the docks?"

"The docks?" Sniffles' eyes widened, and he took a half-step back. "I mean, uh, not much. Just your typical fishy business, right? Nothing a hound like you needs to worry about."

Rex took a deliberate step forward, looming over the smaller dog. "I don't have time for games, Sniffles. I caught a scent at the penthouse that's leading me straight to the docks, and if you've got anything useful rattling around in that nervous little head of yours, now's the time to spill."

Sniffles swallowed hard, his gaze darting to the alley's exit like a cornered mouse looking for an escape. "Alright, alright!" he stammered. "Look, I don't know much, okay? Just... whispers. Word is, the Cartel's been sniffing around the docks more than usual. Something about a big score."

"A big score," Rex repeated, his tone flat. "That's all you've got?"

"I swear!" Sniffles raised his paws defensively. "I don't poke my nose where it doesn't belong, Rex. Not with those cats. Mittens Malone doesn't exactly play nice."

Rex's nose twitched, the scent of fish oil tugging at his instincts like a leash. "This 'big score' wouldn't happen to involve a diamond-encrusted bone, would it?"

Sniffles' eyes widened again, his reaction answering the question before his words could. "The bone? You mean... you're on *that* case?"

"I'm asking the questions, Sniffles," Rex growled. "What do you know about the bone?"

"Not much!" Sniffles insisted, his voice rising in pitch. "Just that it's... valuable. More than it looks, you know? But if the Cartel's involved, it's bad news, Rex. Real bad. They don't mess around."

Rex let the silence hang for a moment, his sharp gaze pinning Sniffles in place. Finally, he stepped back, his posture relaxing just enough to let the Chihuahua breathe. "Thanks for the warning," he said, his tone neutral. "Now do me a favor—stay out of my way."

Sniffles nodded furiously, backing toward the shadows. "Sure thing, Rex. You, uh... take care of yourself, alright? Those cats don't like dogs snooping around."

"They don't like a lot of things," Rex muttered as Sniffles scurried away. He adjusted his hat, his ears twitching at the distant hum of the docks. The scent was stronger now, mingling with the salt and diesel in the air. It wasn't just fish oil—it was something darker, sharper, a promise of trouble waiting to be uncovered.

Rex set off again, his boots splashing through the rain-slicked streets. The docks loomed closer with every step, their shadows stretching out like the city's crooked fingers. If the Cartel was behind the robbery, they'd left the scent for a reason. Whether it was a warning or a trap, Rex was about to find out.

"Fish oil, muddy pawprints, and a nervous Chihuahua," Rex muttered to himself. "This trail's starting to stink worse than the docks."

The rain hadn't let up, its rhythm now a steady percussion against the worn brick walls of Barkington's narrow streets. Rex Barkley moved like a shadow, his boots striking the slick pavement with deliberate intent. The air here was heavy with damp and diesel fumes, tinged with a faint brine that only grew stronger as he neared the docks. His nose twitched, the trail of fish oil still fresh in his mind, mingling with the distant hum of dockside machinery.

He rounded a corner into an alley that smelled worse than it looked, and it looked bad—overflowing trash bins, walls slick with grime, and a few rats scurrying for cover as Rex's imposing figure blocked out the dim streetlight. He stopped halfway down, his ears perking at the sound of faint rustling behind a stack of wooden pallets.

"Alright," Rex said, his gravelly voice cutting through the rain-soaked quiet. "I know you're there. Come out before I drag you out."

For a moment, nothing moved. Then, with the kind of exaggerated care only someone terrified could muster, a wiry alley cat slinked out from the shadows. He was scrawny, with patchy fur and eyes that darted like moths around a flame. His tail twitched nervously as he took a tentative step forward.

"Easy, Detective," the cat said, raising a paw in mock surrender. "No need to get your hackles up."

"Patch," Rex muttered, his eyes narrowing. "Figures I'd find you here. This alley's got your stink all over it."

Patch gave a weak grin, his crooked teeth catching the faint light. "Gotta stay where the action is, don't I? You wouldn't want me in one of those fancy districts, scaring the fine folks."

Rex didn't return the smile. Instead, he stepped closer, looming over the smaller creature. "What do you know about the docks?"

Patch's grin faltered, his ears flattening as he shuffled back a step. "The docks? Nah, not my scene, Detective. Too wet for my taste."

"Don't play dumb," Rex growled. "I caught a trail that leads straight there. Fish oil, muddy pawprints. And if there's one place in this city that reeks of both, it's the docks."

Patch swallowed, his tail flicking nervously. "Look, I hear things, sure. But that doesn't mean I go sniffing around where I don't belong. The Cartel—"

"So it *is* the Cartel," Rex cut in, his voice low and sharp. "They're involved, aren't they?"

Patch winced, glancing toward the mouth of the alley as though expecting someone to appear. "Keep your voice down," he hissed. "You think those cats don't have ears everywhere? You say their name too loud, and you'll wish you hadn't."

"I'll take my chances," Rex said, stepping closer. "Talk."

Patch hesitated, his eyes darting back to Rex's face. The bloodhound's unflinching stare bore into him, and finally, the cat sighed, his shoulders sagging in defeat. "Alright, alright. I've heard whispers. Something big's going down at the docks—something the Cartel doesn't want anyone sticking their noses in."

Rex folded his arms. "What kind of 'something'?"

Patch shook his head, his fur bristling as though the words themselves were dangerous. "I don't know the details, okay? Just that they're on edge. More patrols, more meetings, less room for guys like me to scrounge without getting clawed."

"And the bone?" Rex pressed, his tone steady but insistent. "Does this 'something' have anything to do with a diamond-encrusted chew toy?"

Patch blinked, his nervous energy briefly replaced by confusion. "Bone? What bone?"

"You're telling me you haven't heard a word about it?" Rex asked, his ears tilting slightly forward. "Not even a whisper?"

"Not until now," Patch said, holding up his paws. "If the Cartel's got a shiny toy, they're keeping it under wraps. Maybe it's part of the deal they're cooking, maybe not. I don't know."

Rex let the silence linger, watching the way Patch's tail flicked, his claws flexing slightly against the ground. The cat wasn't lying—at least, not entirely—but there was more he wasn't saying. Rex's nose twitched, catching the faintest whiff of fear mixed with cheap fish.

"You're scared," Rex said finally, his tone flat. "More than usual. Why?"

Patch hesitated, his gaze darting to the alley's mouth again. "Because you don't mess with the Cartel, Detective. Not if you value your tail. They don't care who you are or what you know—they make you disappear all the same."

"I'm not scared of a few alley cats playing king of the hill," Rex replied, his voice edged with steel. "If they've got the bone, I'll find it."

Patch let out a hollow laugh, shaking his head. "You don't get it, do you? This isn't just another job for you, Rex. You go poking around the docks, and you're not coming back with just a story. You're coming back in pieces—if you're lucky."

"Appreciate the concern," Rex said dryly, turning to leave. "But I've got a case to solve."

"Hey!" Patch called after him, his voice cracking slightly. "You think you're untouchable? You think the Cartel's just gonna let you walk into their den? You're gonna end up as a warning, Rex."

Rex paused, glancing over his shoulder. "If they wanted to warn me, they'd have sent someone scarier than you."

Patch scowled, but he didn't argue. As Rex stepped out of the alley and back into the rain, the faint scent of fish oil tugged at his nose once more. The docks were waiting, and so was trouble.

"Warnings," Rex muttered under his breath. "Never been much for heeding them."

The rain continued its relentless rhythm, each droplet cascading off Rex Barkley's fedora as he stood at the edge of the dimly lit street, staring down the distant glow of Barkington's docks. The faint scent of fish oil lingered, pulling at him like an invisible tether. He rubbed his chin, his coarse paw brushing against the worn edge of his trench coat. Patch's warning echoed in his mind, but it wasn't fear that tugged at his gut. It was something deeper—an itch he couldn't scratch, a question that demanded an answer.

"Don't mess with the Cartel," Rex muttered under his breath, his voice heavy with sarcasm. "Great advice from someone who can't even mess with a trash can without getting chased off."

His eyes narrowed as he turned his gaze to the docks. The shadows seemed alive, shifting and moving with the pulse of dockside activity. Forklifts rumbled in the distance, their headlights cutting through the mist. Figures moved like phantoms among the warehouses, shrouded by the oppressive darkness. If the Alley Cartel was cooking something up here, it wasn't going to wait for daylight.

Rex adjusted his coat, his claws brushing against the edge of his pocket where his notebook rested. This wasn't about the money—not anymore. Sure, the promised payout was tempting, but it wasn't what drove him forward. It was the challenge, the thrill of unraveling a knot no one else could untangle. And maybe—just maybe—it was about proving to himself that he still had what it took. That he wasn't just another washed-up mutt clinging to the scraps of his former glory.

With a resolute sigh, he stepped off the curb, his boots splashing through the shallow puddles that littered the street. As he made his way toward the docks, the faint hum of distant voices reached his ears, carried by the wind.

"...shipment's late," one voice grumbled, low and irritated.

"It's the weather," another replied, sharper. "You think the boss doesn't know that? Keep your ears up and your mouth shut."

Rex slowed his pace, his keen ears swiveling toward the source of the voices. He slipped into the shadows, pressing himself against the slick brick wall of a nearby warehouse. Peeking around the corner, he spotted two figures—a stout bulldog with a thick scar across his muzzle and a lanky tabby with a twitchy tail. Both wore the kind of expressions that told Rex they weren't here to exchange pleasantries.

"Fish oil," Rex whispered to himself, catching the faint scent wafting from the crates stacked nearby. The trail was getting stronger.

The bulldog grunted, his paw tapping against the crate he leaned on. "This ain't right. We're drawing too much attention."

The tabby hissed, his tail lashing. "It's not our call. We do what we're told. You want to take it up with Mittens, be my guest."

Mittens. The name hung in the air like a loaded gun. Rex's jaw tightened as he listened, his mind piecing together the fragments of information. Mittens Malone wasn't just a name in this game—he was the game. If the Cartel was behind the theft of Miss Whiskers' precious bone, Mittens would know. And Rex intended to ask him—politely or otherwise.

The tabby flicked his ear, glancing toward the shadows. "You feel that?" he muttered, his voice suddenly uneasy. "Like we're being watched."

Rex froze, his paw instinctively reaching for the small flashlight clipped to his coat. The bulldog stiffened, his scarred muzzle twisting into a snarl. "Ain't nobody stupid enough to come sniffing around here."

"Don't be so sure," the tabby whispered, his eyes narrowing.

Rex stepped back, retreating into the deeper shadows. His breath came slow and steady, his ears tuned to the soft rustle of the wind and the steady rhythm of his own heartbeat. He waited until the pair turned their attention back to the crates, their conversation resuming in hushed tones.

"That's my cue," Rex muttered, slipping away as quietly as he had come.

He moved deeper into the docks, weaving through the maze of warehouses and stacked shipping containers. Each step brought him closer to the heart of the operation, and with it, the answers he sought. The scent of fish oil grew stronger, mingling with the pungent aroma of saltwater and rust. The docks were alive with activity, but it was a careful kind of life— one that thrived in the shadows and shrank from the light.

Rex's resolve hardened with every step. This wasn't just about a stolen bone. It was about something bigger, something that reeked of power plays and hidden agendas. Miss Whiskers had called him in to recover an heirloom, but she hadn't told him everything. She'd left out the part about the Cartel, about the glyph etched into her floor, about the trail that led to Barkington's underbelly.

And that was fine. Rex didn't mind playing the fool if it got him closer to the truth.

As he approached the largest warehouse, its corrugated metal walls looming like a fortress in the mist, Rex paused. The faint murmur of voices reached his ears again, but this time they were accompanied by something else—the sound of a heavy door creaking open.

"Time to see what the Cartel's hiding," he whispered to himself, his tail flicking as he stepped toward the shadows.

The rain pelted him harder as if trying to dissuade him, but Rex pressed on. This was more than a job now. It was a puzzle, and he wouldn't rest until he'd put all the pieces together. His curiosity burned brighter than the warnings Patch and every instinct screamed at him. He was in too deep now, and there was no turning back.

"Curiosity killed the cat," Rex muttered, his voice dry as he approached the warehouse. "Good thing I'm a dog."

Chapter 3
Ambush in the Alley

The rain had slackened to a cold drizzle by the time Rex Barkley turned into the alley shortcut leading to the docks. The neon buzz of a nearby fish market sign lit the narrow passage with a sickly green hue, casting shadows that danced and shifted with every flicker. Rex's coat was damp, his hat pulled low, but his senses were razor-sharp. The scent of fish oil was still there, faint but steady, guiding him closer to Barkington's underbelly.

The alley stretched ahead, a tunnel of slick brick walls and scattered trash. Rex's boots splashed through shallow puddles as his ears pricked at every sound—the distant hum of a streetlamp, the rhythmic drip of water from an overhang. Something felt off. The air was too still, the shadows too alive. He slowed his pace, his nose twitching as he caught the faintest whiff of wet fur and stale cigarettes.

"That's close enough, hound."

The voice was low and gravelly, cutting through the quiet like a shard of glass. Rex stopped, his eyes narrowing as three figures emerged from the shadows ahead. A burly Rottweiler led the pack, his shoulders broad enough to block most of the alley. Flanking him were a wiry tabby and a scrappy terrier, both wearing matching sneers.

"Evening, gentlemen," Rex said, his tone dry but calm. "If this is your idea of a welcoming committee, I've seen friendlier."

The Rottweiler grunted, his eyes cold and calculating. "You've been sticking your nose where it doesn't belong, Barkley."

Rex tilted his head, his paw brushing the edge of his coat. "Funny, I don't remember signing up for the Cartel's etiquette class. What's the matter? I sniffed out something you didn't want me to?"

"Watch your mouth, hound," the terrier snarled, his fur bristling. "You're in deep enough already."

Rex smirked, though his muscles tensed beneath his coat. "Deep enough to make you crawl out of your hole on a rainy night? I must be doing something right."

The tabby hissed, stepping forward with claws unsheathed. "Shut it, Barkley. We don't need you poking around the docks, and we sure as hell don't need you sniffing after the boss's business."

"Your boss must be real nervous if he sent the three stooges to deal with me," Rex quipped, his eyes flicking between them. "What's the matter? Can't handle one dog without backup?"

The Rottweiler growled, his patience clearly wearing thin. "We're here to deliver a message. Back off, or you won't just be limping home next time."

Rex's smirk faded, replaced by a cold, hard stare. "If your boss wanted to send a message, he should've written it himself. Now get out of my way."

The Rottweiler bared his teeth, and for a moment, the alley was silent but for the rain tapping against the walls. Then, with a low snarl, the big dog lunged, his massive frame barreling toward Rex like a freight train.

Rex sidestepped at the last second, his movements quick and practiced. The Rottweiler slammed into the wall with a grunt, but the terrier was already closing in, teeth bared and claws flashing. Rex ducked under the attack, his fist connecting with the terrier's gut in a sharp, precise jab that sent the smaller dog stumbling back.

"You should've stayed home," Rex muttered, spinning to face the tabby. The cat leaped at him with a hiss, his claws aimed for Rex's face. Rex caught the tabby mid-air, slamming him down onto the wet pavement with a grunt of effort.

But the Rottweiler wasn't done. He came at Rex again, this time swinging a heavy paw that caught the detective on the shoulder. Pain shot through Rex's arm, but he gritted his teeth and countered with a swift uppercut that sent the big dog reeling.

The terrier recovered quickly, lunging at Rex's legs in an attempt to bring him down. Rex staggered but managed to kick the smaller dog away, sending him skidding into a pile of trash. The tabby scrambled to his feet, blood dripping from a cut above his eye, and darted back into the fray.

"You're persistent," Rex grunted, dodging the tabby's claws. "I'll give you that."

The fight was brutal and unrelenting, the narrow alley offering little room for maneuvering. Rex took a few hits—his side ached where the Rottweiler had landed a solid blow, and his shoulder throbbed—but he gave as good as he got. His fists flew with precision, each strike landing with a satisfying thud.

Finally, the three thugs retreated, their snarls and hisses replaced by ragged breaths and low growls. The Rottweiler wiped blood from his muzzle, his eyes burning with fury. "You got lucky, hound."

"Lucky?" Rex spat, his voice steady despite the pain. "You think this is luck? Go back to your boss and tell him Rex Barkley doesn't scare easy."

The Rottweiler growled but said nothing, jerking his head at his companions. The trio slinked back into the shadows, their forms disappearing into the rain.

Rex leaned against the wall, catching his breath. His coat was torn, his hat askew, but he was still standing. He glanced down at his paw, flexing his fingers. A small slip of fabric clung to his claws—fish-scented and damp. A clue.

"Looks like your message got lost in translation," Rex muttered, straightening his coat. His injuries ached, but his resolve burned brighter than ever. The docks were waiting, and so were the answers he needed.

With one last glance down the alley, Rex adjusted his hat and stepped forward into the rain.

The rain fell harder as Rex straightened himself against the alley wall, his breaths coming in shallow gasps. His trench coat was torn at the shoulder, and his hat sat at a crooked angle, but he was still standing, and that counted for something. The thugs had slunk away, tails between their legs, but their parting growls echoed in his ears. His side throbbed where the Rottweiler had landed a solid blow, but the ache was muted by something sharper—curiosity.

Rex glanced down at his paw, where a damp scrap of fabric clung to his claws. The faint scent of fish oil wafted up, cutting through the pungent cocktail of wet fur and alley grime. He brought the fabric closer to his nose, sniffing with the precision only a bloodhound could manage. It was faint, but the smell was unmistakable—a salty tang mixed with the sharp bite of something industrial. It reeked of the docks.

"Fish oil again," Rex muttered, turning the scrap over in his paw. It was frayed along one edge, as if torn in a scuffle. "What are you trying to tell me, Mittens?"

He crouched low to the ground, scanning the scene for anything the rain hadn't washed away yet. The scuffle had churned up the puddles and scattered trash across the alley, but Rex's sharp eyes caught the faint outline of pawprints leading toward the docks. His ears twitched, straining to pick up any distant sounds over the steady drum of rain.

Then, buried under the scattered debris, something glinted in the dim neon glow of a nearby sign. Rex reached out, brushing aside a soggy paper wrapper to reveal a small metallic pin shaped like a stylized claw. He held it up to the light, turning it between his fingers. It was cheap, the kind of trinket you'd expect from a gang looking to mark its members.

"The Alley Cartel's calling card," he murmured, his lips curling into a grim smile. "You boys aren't subtle, are you?"

As he stood, the sound of a bottle clattering against the pavement made him whip around. His paw hovered near his coat pocket, ready to draw... nothing. He grimaced. He wasn't the kind of dog to carry heat, but moments like this made him wish he were.

"Who's there?" he barked, his tone sharp enough to cut through the rain.

A figure emerged from the shadows, small and wiry, with fur slicked down from the rain. It was Sniffles McGruff, his oversized trench coat dripping as he held his paws up defensively.

"Relax, Rex, it's just me!" Sniffles squeaked, his voice cracking. "Don't go biting my head off."

Rex lowered his guard slightly, his eyes narrowing. "Sniffles, what are you doing skulking around here? Thought I told you to stay out of my way."

"I wasn't skulking," Sniffles protested, shuffling closer. "I was... checking on you. Heard some noise, figured you could use a paw."

Rex snorted, shoving the metallic pin into his coat pocket. "Sure you did. You hear anything useful while you were 'checking on me,' or are you just here for the show?"

Sniffles fidgeted, his tail curling around his leg. "Alright, alright. I might've overheard something. Those guys who jumped you? They're low-level muscle for the Cartel. They don't make moves unless someone higher up gives the order."

"No kidding," Rex said dryly, gesturing to his torn coat. "Got the memo loud and clear. Anything else?"

"Yeah," Sniffles said, his voice dropping to a conspiratorial whisper. "Word is, they've been getting restless lately. Something about a big job going sideways. Rumor has it, the boss isn't happy."

Rex's ears perked at that, his mind churning. A big job going sideways could mean anything, but combined with the staged robbery at Miss Whiskers' penthouse, it painted a picture he didn't like. "You hear anything about a diamond-encrusted bone?" he asked, watching Sniffles closely.

The Chihuahua's eyes widened, his expression shifting to something between fear and confusion. "The bone? You think that's what this is about?"

"I don't think," Rex said, stepping closer. "I *know*. And if the Cartel's involved, that means someone at the top has a reason to keep it quiet."

Sniffles hesitated, his gaze darting to the alley's mouth as though he expected someone to appear. "Look, Rex, you're playing with fire here. The Cartel doesn't mess around, and neither does Mittens. If you're smart, you'll walk away before you end up in a trash heap."

"Smart doesn't pay the bills," Rex muttered, brushing past him. "Stay out of trouble, Sniffles."

As Rex stepped back into the rain, his thoughts churned like the storm clouds overhead. The metallic pin and fish-scented fabric felt like puzzle pieces, each hinting at a bigger picture he couldn't see yet. The pawprints, the staged robbery, the bone— it all tied back to the Cartel. And if Mittens Malone was pulling the strings, Rex needed to get to him before the trail went cold.

He paused at the edge of the alley, pulling the fabric scrap from his pocket again. The faint scent of fish oil lingered, pulling him toward the docks like an invisible leash. The Cartel had tried to warn him off, but they'd only made him more determined.

"You wanted me to back off," Rex muttered, his voice low and edged with defiance. "Guess you don't know me very well."

Adjusting his hat, Rex stepped into the misty glow of the streetlights, his silhouette fading into the rain. The docks were waiting, and so were the answers he needed.

The rain beat down harder as Rex Barkley emerged from the alley, his trench coat clinging to his frame and his hat drooping under the weight of the storm. The sharp ache in his ribs reminded him of the Rottweiler's earlier punch, but it wasn't enough to slow him down. Pain was a constant companion in his line of work, but curiosity—curiosity was the motivator. And right now, it was burning brighter than the streetlights flickering in the rain.

The docks loomed ahead, their shadows stretching long and dark like the claws of the city's underbelly. Forklifts hummed in the distance, and the faint cries of gulls mixed with the relentless tap of rain on corrugated metal. Rex's nose twitched; the scent of fish oil was unmistakable now, stronger with every step.

As he approached the outer perimeter, he slipped into the shadows cast by a stack of abandoned crates. His breath was steady, despite the ache in his side, and his sharp eyes scanned the scene. Figures moved in and out of a large warehouse, their forms blurred by the mist and rain. A pair of cats stood by the entrance, their postures tense and watchful, clearly on guard.

"Looks like the Cartel's rolling out the red carpet," Rex muttered under his breath.

He leaned back against the crates, debating his next move. Every instinct screamed at him to approach cautiously—these weren't the kind of cats who asked questions first. But hesitation wasn't his style, and the trail he was following led straight into the lion's den.

A faint shuffle behind him made his ears twitch. He turned just in time to see Sniffles McGruff slinking toward him, his oversized trench coat dripping and his tail curled tight against his body.

"Sniffles," Rex growled. "What part of 'stay out of trouble' did you not understand?"

Sniffles froze, his ears flattening as he raised his paws defensively. "I wasn't following you, honest! I just... figured you might need some backup."

Rex sighed, pinching the bridge of his nose. "Backup? From you? I just spent five minutes mopping up three Cartel thugs in an alley. What are you gonna do—bore them to death with your excuses?"

"I'm serious!" Sniffles whispered, his voice low but urgent. "You think you're the only one who wants to see the Cartel taken down? They've been running this part of the city for years, Rex. Someone's gotta stand up to them."

Rex studied the smaller dog for a moment, his expression unreadable. "Fine," he said finally, his tone begrudging. "But stay out of my way. You so much as sneeze loud enough to get us caught, and I'll leave you to explain yourself to Mittens."

Sniffles gulped but nodded, his nervous energy palpable. "Got it. Silent as a mouse."

Rex turned his attention back to the warehouse. The guards by the door were chatting now, their voices low but audible over the rain. He caught snippets of their conversation, just enough to make out the tone—impatience mixed with a hint of unease. Something was happening inside, something big enough to have the Alley Cartel on edge.

"I need to get closer," Rex muttered.

"What's the plan?" Sniffles asked, craning his neck to peer around the crates.

"You're staying here," Rex said, his voice firm. "If this goes sideways, I don't need you dragging me down."

"But—" Sniffles began, only to be silenced by a sharp glare from Rex.

"No buts," Rex snapped. "You want to help? Keep watch. If anyone comes this way, make some noise. Otherwise, stay out of sight."

Sniffles looked like he wanted to argue but thought better of it. He nodded reluctantly, retreating a few steps into the shadows.

Satisfied, Rex moved toward the warehouse, his steps careful and deliberate. The rain provided cover, masking the sound of his movements as he closed the distance to the side of the building. He flattened himself against the wall, his ears straining to catch the voices inside.

"You think the boss'll be here tonight?" one of the guards asked, his tone nervous.

"Doubt it," the other replied. "He doesn't get his paws dirty unless he has to. This is just cleanup."

Cleanup. The word stuck in Rex's mind like a thorn. Whatever was happening inside wasn't just a transaction—it was damage control. And that meant the Cartel had something to hide.

Rex edged closer to a cracked window, peering inside. The interior of the warehouse was dimly lit, its vast space filled with crates and barrels. A group of cats was clustered near the center, their attention focused on a table piled high with papers and what looked like blueprints. At the edge of the scene stood a familiar figure—a Rottweiler with a scarred muzzle, the same thug who had ambushed Rex in the alley.

"Well, well," Rex murmured. "Looks like you boys brought me a lead after all."

The scent of fish oil was overwhelming now, and Rex's eyes landed on a stack of crates near the table, each one stamped with a logo that matched the glyph he'd seen in Miss Whiskers' penthouse. His jaw tightened. The connection was clear now— the Cartel wasn't just behind the robbery. They were orchestrating something much bigger.

"Rex?" Sniffles' voice hissed from behind him, barely audible. "You okay?"

Rex turned slightly, his expression hard but determined. "I'm better than okay," he whispered. "I've got what I need."

"What do we do now?" Sniffles asked, his voice trembling slightly.

Rex adjusted his hat, the faintest hint of a smile tugging at the corner of his mouth. "We do what I do best, Sniffles. We follow the trail, and we make some noise."

Despite the odds stacked against him, Rex felt his resolve strengthen. The pain in his ribs, the rain soaking through his coat, the lingering threat of the Cartel—it all faded into the background. He wasn't just chasing a case anymore. He was chasing the truth. And no amount of rain or muscle was going to stop him.

Chapter 4
Pawprints in the Shadows

The stench hit Rex Barkley before he even turned the corner: sardines, saltwater, and something faintly rancid—like time itself had given up and rotted. The Barkington fish market was a sprawling, grimy warehouse down by the docks, where the air clung to you like an unwelcome second coat. This late at night, the place was half-empty, lit only by flickering overhead bulbs that buzzed like they resented still being alive.

Rex shoved his way through the front doors, his limp more noticeable after the night's earlier run-ins. His coat hung heavy, his hat casting his eyes into shadow. Still, he moved like he owned the room—or at least wasn't afraid to tear it apart.

The cats were waiting for him.

At the far end of the market, a small empire of crates had been built into something resembling a throne room. Cats lounged on barrels and wooden pallets, all of them low-slung and watching him with unblinking eyes. At the center, draped lazily over a crate like royalty, was Mittens Malone.

Mittens was everything Rex expected—bigger than most tabbies, broad-shouldered with a scar that split one ear clean in half. His fur was sleek but unkempt, giving him the look of someone who didn't care what you thought so long as you knew to stay out of his way. He licked his paw once, lazily, and watched Rex approach like a lion watches a slow-moving gazelle.

"Well, well," Mittens drawled, his voice deep and smooth as molasses. "If it isn't Barkington's least-loved bloodhound. You lose your nose, or are you just looking for a place to curl up and die?"

"Funny," Rex said, coming to a stop just short of Mittens' court. "I didn't think cats were supposed to laugh with their mouths full."

Mittens' smirk froze. Rex's gaze flicked to the sardine crate Mittens leaned against, still half-open, its silvery contents reeking of brine.

"Looks like you've been eating well, Mittens," Rex continued, his voice low and steady. "You always this generous with the crew, or is this special delivery just for you?"

Mittens' tail swished lazily, but the sharp glint in his yellow eyes gave him away. "You've got a real habit of sticking your snout where it doesn't belong, hound."

"That's what they tell me," Rex replied. "But we both know I don't follow habits—I follow scents. And the scent of this case brought me straight to you."

Mittens sat up straighter, his paws settling against the edge of the crate. The cats around him stiffened, their claws twitching against the wood. "Is that so?"

"That's so," Rex said, unbuttoning his coat just enough to look comfortable. "The diamond-encrusted bone. I've got a client who thinks you—or your crew—had something to do with it going missing. What do you say to that?"

Mittens let out a low, gruff laugh, like gravel tumbling downhill. "You came all the way down here to accuse me of lifting some glittery chew toy? Barkley, I'm insulted. I don't deal in bones—especially not ones dripping with dog slobber."

"Didn't say *you* took it," Rex replied, taking a step forward. "But someone's playing games with that bone, and they're tying your name to it. Makes you look sloppy. Thought you'd want to set the record straight."

The room went still for a beat. Mittens' gaze didn't waver, though his tail thumped once, slow and deliberate. "I don't do sloppy, Barkley. And I don't answer to you."

Rex tilted his head. "Then maybe you'll answer to someone else. Miss Whiskers, for example?"

The reaction was slight—just the briefest twitch of Mittens' whiskers—but Rex caught it. Mittens' claws flexed against the crate, his expression turning cold. "Miss Whiskers," he repeated, as though tasting the name. "Now there's a cat who likes to land on her feet, no matter who she pushes off the ledge to get there."

"So you do know something," Rex said. "I'll bet you two go way back. You help her with this little performance, Mittens?

Break a window, plant some pawprints—maybe you two are splitting the profits?"

Mittens hissed softly, rising to his full height, his voice a low growl. "You don't know a thing about her. That Siamese has claws you don't see until it's too late. If she's dangling you by the tail, then you've already lost."

Rex narrowed his eyes, unflinching as Mittens loomed over him. "She says you've got it out for her. Makes me wonder what's between you two and that bone."

"The bone's not what you think," Mittens snapped, his voice sharp enough to make his crew shift uneasily. "It's more than some jewel-encrusted chewable. If Miss Whiskers wants it back, it ain't because of sentiment."

The words hung in the air like a blade, and Rex's ears perked. He'd poked something now—something buried deeper than Mittens wanted to admit.

"Then what is it?" Rex asked, his tone even but pressing. "What's the bone really worth?"

Mittens didn't answer right away. He stared at Rex, his gaze calculating, dangerous. Then he leaned closer, close enough that Rex could smell sardines and the faint metallic tinge of blood on his breath.

"You keep chasing this trail, hound, you're gonna find out the hard way," Mittens said, his voice a low rumble. "The kind of truth you don't walk away from."

"I'll take my chances," Rex replied, not blinking. "But you've got your own problems, don't you, Mittens? Someone's trying to stir up trouble, and it's got your name on it. Maybe Miss Whiskers. Maybe someone else. Either way, they're making you look weak."

The tabby's tail thumped again, harder this time, his patience clearly fraying. "You want advice, Barkley? Get out while you still can. No one comes out clean when the Alley Cartel's involved."

"Clean's not my style," Rex shot back. "But I'll keep that in mind."

Mittens didn't respond. He flicked a paw, and the cats lounging nearby sprang to attention, their bodies tensed, ready to pounce. Rex got the message. The conversation was over.

He turned, limping back through the maze of crates, his nose still twitching with the stink of fish and lies. Mittens' words echoed in his ears, gnawing at him like a bone left half-buried: *"The bone's not what you think."*

It wasn't just a missing heirloom. It was something bigger. Something worth spilling blood over. And if Miss Whiskers was at the center of it, Rex knew one thing for certain—he'd have to dig deeper than ever to find the truth.

As he stepped back into the rain-soaked night, Rex pulled his collar up and muttered to himself, "Careful, Mittens. I don't spook easy, and this hound's got a nose for trouble."

The fish market's stench still clung to Rex Barkley's coat as he paused near a stack of crates. Mittens Malone was pacing now, the flick of his tail a metronome ticking to the beat of his growing frustration. Around them, the feline thugs watched with unblinking eyes, their claws twitching against wood and stone. Rex stayed put, hands in his coat pockets, hat brim low enough to hide the glint in his eyes. If Mittens was about to crack, Rex wasn't going to rush him.

"Funny thing about Miss Whiskers," Mittens said finally, his voice tight, like he was holding back more than words. "Everyone sees the fur, the charm, the diamond collar. The kind of cat who lands on her feet every time, right?"

"That's the rumor," Rex replied, his tone even. "She wears it well."

Mittens scoffed, his sharp teeth flashing under the buzzing overhead light. "She doesn't just land on her feet. She climbs her way up on *your* back and leaves the claw marks as a souvenir."

"That so?" Rex tilted his head, just enough to show he was listening. "Sounds personal."

Mittens froze mid-pace, his yellow eyes narrowing into slits. "You think I'm venting? That I'm sittin' here cryin' over spilled milk? I don't get sentimental, Barkley. Not about her."

"Sure you don't," Rex said, letting the faintest edge creep into his voice. "That's why you're pacing like you've got fleas under your fur."

Mittens' ears flattened for half a second before he forced himself still, smoothing his expression back into something cold and controlled. But Rex had seen the crack, and Mittens knew it. He sighed heavily, like he was about to spit out a bone that had been stuck for years.

"You want the truth? Fine." Mittens stepped closer, close enough that Rex caught the faint musk of old sweat and fish oil. "Me and Miss Whiskers—we go back. Way back. Back to when this city still had rules."

Rex raised an eyebrow. "Sounds like storytime. Enlighten me."

Mittens' claws flexed against the crate, his tail swishing hard enough to make the thugs nearby flinch. "She wasn't always dripping diamonds and walking around like she owned the place. We were partners once—smuggling, mostly. Goods that moved easier when no one asked questions."

"What goods?"

"Catnip. Crystals. The shiny stuff that makes the alley rats twitch," Mittens said, his voice low and dark. "But that was just the start. Miss Whiskers? She had ambition. More than most cats have brains."

Rex nodded, filing it all away. "And you let her call the shots?"

Mittens' eyes flashed. "No one *lets* Miss Whiskers do anything. You think you're playing her game, but it's always hers, start to finish. She'd get you to move the pieces, make you think you were winning—then she'd swipe the whole board out from under you. I learned that the hard way."

Rex folded his arms across his chest. "What happened?"

Mittens paused, staring past Rex like he was seeing something far older than the crates and fish market walls. When he spoke again, his voice had an edge of bitterness. "There was a job. Big shipment, high stakes. Smuggling jewels from across the river. The kind of deal that could set you up for life if you didn't screw it up."

"And let me guess—things went sour."

Mittens snapped his gaze back to Rex, his face twisted into a sneer. "Not on my end. I had the plan, I had the crew. All she had to do was play her part. But she turned on us—flipped the job at the last minute. Took the jewels, took the credits, left us sitting there looking like fools when the heat came down."

Rex's nose twitched. The pieces were clicking into place, but the story still had holes. "She double-crossed you," Rex said slowly. "And you've been chasing that ever since."

Mittens' laugh was sharp and humorless. "Chasing it? No, Barkley. I cut my losses. You don't chase a cat like her unless you're ready to lose everything."

Rex studied him for a moment, his instincts humming. Mittens was trying to play it cool, but the flick of his tail and the tension in his shoulders told a different story. There was more here—bad blood that went deeper than just a double-cross.

"So why do you care now?" Rex pressed. "If she's such a lost cause, why bother with this bone business?"

Mittens' expression darkened, his claws sinking into the wood beneath him. "Because whatever she's wrapped up in now, it's bigger than her usual cons. She doesn't make moves unless there's something *worth* moving for, and you'd better believe if Miss Whiskers wants that bone, it ain't just about sentiment."

"Then what's it about?" Rex asked, his tone hardening. "You seem to know more than you're letting on."

Mittens leaned in, his voice dropping to a low growl. "If I knew, I'd be sitting pretty instead of watching half this city sniff around like rats in the dark. But here's a freebie for you, Barkley: that bone's not just a jewel-encrusted chew toy. It's leverage—old leverage. The kind of thing that turns rivals into corpses and friends into liars."

Rex's brow furrowed, the weight of Mittens' words settling on him like cold rain. "And what's your play in all this, Malone?"

Mittens stepped back, his smirk returning like a mask sliding into place. "My play? I'm just a cat trying to keep his tail out of the fire. You want to play hero, that's on you. But if you stick your nose where it doesn't belong, you'll find out the hard way just how sharp Whiskers' claws really are."

Rex watched him for a long moment, his mind turning over every word. Mittens Malone might've been a liar, a thief, and a thug, but the fear behind his arrogance wasn't fake. He knew something—or had seen something—that made him want no part of this mess.

Rex adjusted his hat and turned toward the warehouse door, the scent of fish oil and trouble lingering on the air. "I'll keep that in mind," he said over his shoulder. "But if Whiskers' claws are as sharp as you say, you might wanna watch your own tail, Mittens. You're already bleeding."

Mittens didn't respond, just watched Rex disappear into the rain, his eyes glinting like two pale coins in the dark. Whatever history Mittens had with Miss Whiskers, it was clear he'd been burned before. And now Rex Barkley was walking into the same fire.

He just hoped he didn't come out singed.

Rex Barkley's boots echoed against the damp warehouse floor as he turned for the exit. The fish market felt heavier now, like the air had thickened with the weight of what Mittens Malone had said. Smuggling jobs, old grudges, and Miss Whiskers' knack for weaving others into her schemes—it all left a sour taste in Rex's mouth, like day-old kibble washed down with bad coffee.

Behind him, Mittens hadn't moved, still perched on his crate throne, his yellow eyes sharp and fixed on Rex's back. The silence dragged, broken only by the faint slosh of water dripping from a cracked gutter somewhere outside.

"You really think you've got it figured out, don't you?" Mittens' voice cut through the air like a claw across glass.

Rex paused, his hand on the warehouse door. He didn't turn, but the words hung there, daring him to listen. "I figure the truth always smells like something, Malone. I just follow the stink."

A low chuckle rolled from Mittens, dark and humorless. "You're good at that, Barkley. I'll give you that. But for a detective, you've got a real bad habit of missing the big picture."

Rex turned just enough to glance back over his shoulder, his silhouette framed by the hazy light of the docks outside. "You've got something to say, say it. I don't have time for riddles."

Mittens stood slowly, his movements deliberate as he stepped down from his makeshift throne. The sound of his claws tapping against the crate's edge was soft, but it carried a weight that made Rex's ears twitch. "Fine. You want it straight? Here it is."

He stopped a few feet from Rex, his tail curling lazily behind him as his yellow eyes locked onto Rex's. "You think she came to you for help, hound? You think you're some kind of savior?" Mittens' voice dropped, every word deliberate and heavy. "She came to you because she needs a fall guy."

Rex didn't move. He didn't blink, didn't speak, didn't let the words hit him harder than they should've. But Mittens saw the flicker in his eyes, the one thing Rex couldn't hide—doubt.

"You think you're chasing a case, sniffing out a missing bone?" Mittens continued, his tone laced with something halfway between pity and disdain. "You're chasing *her* case, Barkley. She's got you right where she wants you, and by the time you figure that out, you'll already be neck-deep."

"Neck-deep in what?" Rex growled, his voice low and edged with warning.

"Whatever mess she's wrapped up in." Mittens' grin returned, though it lacked its usual smugness. "She's good at spinning webs, that one. She's got claws you don't see coming, and she's already got you tangled. If I were you, I'd take that as a warning."

Rex stepped forward, closing the space between them. Even with his leg throbbing and the exhaustion dragging at him, he stood tall, his bloodhound frame towering over the tabby.

"And if you were me, Mittens, you'd know I don't scare easy. I don't walk away just because someone's leaving pawprints where they shouldn't."

Mittens' smirk twitched, just barely. "Maybe not. But don't say I didn't warn you when she twists that leash around your neck and pulls tight."

For a moment, the two locked eyes—hound and cat, predator and predator, standing still in the damp, cavernous room. Mittens had said his piece, and Rex could feel it burrowing into his thoughts like an itch he couldn't scratch. But he wasn't about to let Malone see that.

"I'll take my chances," Rex muttered, turning back toward the door.

Mittens' voice followed him, echoing softly across the fish-scented air. "You're already taking them, Barkley. You just don't know it yet."

Rex shoved the door open, stepping into the rain-soaked night. The cold air hit him like a slap, washing away the cloying stink of sardines and lies, but not the weight of Mittens' words. *She needs a fall guy.*

The phrase rolled around in his head as he trudged back toward the streets, his limp more pronounced now that the adrenaline was wearing off. The rain drummed against his hat, streaming off the brim in steady rivulets, but Rex barely noticed.

Miss Whiskers had come to him looking like the picture of a helpless client—diamonds, silk, and carefully measured words. But everything about this case had been off since the moment she stepped through his door. The staged robbery. The perfectly planted pawprints. The cryptic glyph scratched into the marble floor.

Rex frowned, his nose twitching at the thought. Mittens wasn't just talking to talk. The tabby might've been a crook, but he wasn't stupid. If he thought Miss Whiskers was up to something, then Rex had to consider the possibility that Malone was right.

"Fall guy," Rex muttered to himself, his voice lost to the rain. "That'd be just my luck."

He stopped at the corner, pulling his coat tighter against the wind. The city stretched out in front of him, dark and endless, its alleys twisting like secrets waiting to be unraveled. Somewhere in all that mess, Miss Whiskers was hiding something—something bigger than a missing bone and more dangerous than Mittens' grudges.

Rex clenched his jaw, the ache in his leg reminding him of just how far he'd already been pulled into this.

"If I'm a fall guy," he said softly, flicking the rain off the brim of his hat, "then someone's gonna regret pushing me."

With that, Rex turned into the night, his boots splashing through puddles as the rain came down harder, hammering the city like a warning that no one was listening to. But Rex wasn't listening either. He was a bloodhound on a scent, and no matter where it led, he wasn't letting go.

Chapter 5
Beneath the Penthouse Glare

The Kennel Club stood out against the drab backdrop of Barkington like a polished bone in a pile of dirt. Its marble facade gleamed under spotlights, and the faint sound of laughter and clinking glasses drifted out into the rain-soaked night. Rex Barkley tilted his hat lower as he stood across the street, half-hidden in the shadow of a lamppost. It was the kind of place that reeked of money, power, and well-fed egos— exactly the kind of place where corruption rubbed elbows with class.

The gala was already in full swing, the crystal chandeliers inside casting a golden glow visible even through the grand windows. Cars pulled up in steady intervals, sleek and spotless, disgorging Barkington's elite—poodles in silk scarves, terriers in fitted tuxedos, and a handful of smug Persians who walked like they owned the floor. Rex's nose twitched. The stink of arrogance carried all the way across the street.

He adjusted the bowtie at his throat, the stiff black fabric foreign and uncomfortable under his trench coat. A disguise wasn't Rex's style—he was a bloodhound who liked to let his nose and trench coat do the talking—but tonight called for something subtler. Beneath his coat, he wore a cheap waiter's vest he'd lifted from a dry cleaner's rack two blocks over.

Rex muttered to himself as he checked the door one last time. "Never thought I'd trade my dignity for a serving tray."

The rain slowed to a mist as Rex crossed the street, his limp hardly noticeable as he fell into step with a group of actual waiters unloading crates of hors d'oeuvres. He grabbed a silver tray from the top of a stack, balancing it just enough to look convincing. The doorman barely glanced at him as he slipped inside, too distracted by the arrival of a particularly loud schnauzer in a ridiculous top hat.

The Kennel Club's main hall was a cathedral of wealth—marble floors so polished they reflected the chandeliers above, walls lined with gilded mirrors, and music drifting from a live quartet tucked into the corner. Dogs and cats of privilege glided across the room, gossiping through smiles and sipping from delicate crystal glasses. Rex moved quietly, tray in paw, letting the flow of the room guide him. He blended in just enough, but his nose worked overtime, cataloging every scent—expensive perfume, brandy, and beneath it all, something darker, murkier.

"Canapés?" Rex mumbled, offering his tray to a pair of Afghan Hounds who barely spared him a glance before drifting toward the auction tables. He frowned, pulling the tray closer. "Didn't want to share anyway."

His eyes flicked across the room, searching. Somewhere in this sea of silk and smug grins were the answers he needed. The Poodle Twins—Baron and Bentley—were at the heart of this gala, throwing around their influence like it was another chew toy they didn't want anyone else to have. The auction was the centerpiece of the night, the bidding an excuse to flaunt power more than to actually collect chewables. Rumor had it they had a paw in every major deal that went sideways in this town—and tonight, Rex was betting someone here knew something about the bone.

His ear twitched as he heard a familiar, purring voice float over the room.

"*Darling,* you can't honestly think that *trinket* is worth ten thousand kibble."

Rex turned just slightly, his eyes locking onto the source. Miss Whiskers. She was perched near the center of the room, holding court beside a table lined with velvet displays. Her diamond collar shimmered under the chandeliers, her silk gown flowing like she'd stepped out of a painting. She smiled, sly and sharp, as she leaned into a smug-looking Siamese tom who was trying too hard to impress her.

Rex muttered to himself, "Of course you're here."

He wove his way through the crowd, pausing just long enough to let the tray of canapés act as camouflage. He caught snippets of conversation as he passed—"My darling terrier won Best in Show *again*..." and "The Poodles are simply *marvelous* for hosting..."—but none of it mattered.

By the time Rex got within earshot, Miss Whiskers was laughing—a soft, practiced sound that dripped charm like honey. "Really, Mr. Chesterfield, you *must* learn when to stop bidding. You wouldn't want to lose your entire estate over a rare chew toy, would you?"

The Siamese tom stammered something incoherent, his ears flushing with embarrassment. Miss Whiskers turned slightly and spotted Rex, her smile faltering just enough for him to notice. Her gaze sharpened, and for a split second, Rex saw the real Miss Whiskers hiding beneath the silk and diamonds.

Rex didn't stop. He moved past her table, pretending not to see her, but he knew she'd caught the scent of him, too. The game had just gotten tighter.

Further down the hall, Rex's nose caught another scent—sardines. Faint, but unmistakable. He followed it to a side corridor where the twins' goons—a pair of slick-coated bulldogs—stood guarding a closed door. Rex didn't slow down. He turned on his heel, grabbed a glass of champagne from another waiter's tray, and worked his way back into the crowd, watching the door from a distance.

"*Psst.*"

The sound came from just behind him. Rex stiffened and turned slightly, finding himself face-to-face with a wiry terrier waiter whose nose was twitching nervously.

"You don't belong here," the terrier muttered, voice low and fast. "I don't know what you're looking for, pal, but you're gonna get yourself buried if you keep sniffing around."

Rex raised an eyebrow, his grip tightening on the tray. "I'm just serving hors d'oeuvres, friend."

The terrier's eyes darted toward the auction tables, then back to Rex. "No one comes here without a reason. And no one leaves without someone noticing. You'd better hope the Twins don't get wind of you, hound. They don't like surprises."

Before Rex could respond, the terrier slipped away, disappearing into the crowd like smoke on a windy night.

Rex glanced back toward the guarded door, the weight of the warning curling in his chest like an itch he couldn't scratch. This gala wasn't just about rare chewables and vanity—it was cover for something bigger. He could feel it in the air, smell it under the perfume and sardines.

As he moved back into the flow of the room, Rex muttered under his breath, "Let 'em notice me. I'm just getting started."

The hum of conversation filled the Kennel Club's grand hall like a low growl beneath the polished refinement. Crystal glasses clinked, laughter rippled, and under the gilded pretense of civility, corruption slithered unseen. Rex Barkley moved carefully, a tray of untouched canapés still balanced in his paw as he let the room guide him. His nose, however, worked double-time, sifting through the scents of perfume, silk, and aged brandy, looking for something—anything—that would point him toward the truth.

His ears perked up as a loud, buttery voice floated across the room. "And here we are, ladies and gentlehounds, the centerpiece of tonight's auction—a legend in its own right!"

Rex turned his head, instincts sharpening like a blade. The voice belonged to Bentley Poodle—half of the Poodle Twins. Bentley stood on a small platform near a velvet-draped auction table, his perfectly groomed curls catching the glow of the chandeliers as he gestured to the crowd with exaggerated flair. Baron Poodle, the quieter of the pair, loomed beside him, a brooding shadow of silent menace.

"Feast your eyes, dear guests," Bentley continued, his voice ringing with theatrical delight, "on this *treasure* of Barkington lore—a photograph of the infamous diamond-encrusted bone."

Rex's eyes locked onto the display as Bentley whipped away a cloth with a dramatic flourish. The crowd murmured, leaning forward to get a better look. The photograph, encased in a gilded frame, sat propped against a velvet stand. The bone in the image glittered like something out of a dream, encrusted with diamonds that caught the light and threw it back tenfold.

Rex's nose twitched. That bone was more than flashy—it was bait.

Bentley let the murmurs swell before he spoke again, leaning closer to the crowd as though sharing a secret. "This precious artifact—long thought lost to the ages—has found its way back to Barkington. Sold to an *anonymous buyer,* naturally."

Rex frowned, his grip tightening on the tray. *Anonymous buyer?* That stank worse than the fish market.

"It's quite the story, really," Bentley went on, his grin all charm and teeth. "A relic of power, passed through generations. But as we all know, the rarest treasures attract… *unseemly interest.*" His voice dipped conspiratorially, sending a ripple through the room.

Rex caught movement out of the corner of his eye—a sleek black Persian whispering something to a terrier in a tuxedo, their eyes darting toward the photograph before slinking back into the shadows. He didn't like the look of it.

"Unseemly interest, huh?" Rex muttered under his breath, maneuvering closer to the edge of the crowd. "Seems like there's plenty of that to go around."

The chatter picked up again as Bentley stepped down, satisfied with the attention he'd drawn. Rex scanned the room, ears tuned for anything worth catching. A snatch of conversation to his right made him pause. Two tuxedo-clad spaniels stood near the punch bowl, heads close together, speaking in low, urgent tones.

"—heard it came through the docks. The Alley Cartel had it first."

Rex stilled, angling his ear subtly toward them.

"You sure?" the other spaniel asked, his brow furrowed. "That's a dangerous game. They don't deal unless there's serious kibble involved."

"Serious kibble and serious strings," the first replied. "Word is, someone paid a fortune to get it out of their paws. Whoever bought it is either crazy or dangerous. Maybe both."

Rex's eyes narrowed. *The docks. The Alley Cartel.* That bone wasn't just a glittery chew toy—it was leverage, just like Mittens had hinted. And if it had already been through the Cartel's claws, there was no telling how deep this went.

He moved closer to the photograph, careful not to draw attention. The bone in the picture practically screamed trouble. Its intricate carvings—symbols and patterns he didn't recognize—were hidden beneath the diamonds, but they told a story. A story that someone didn't want shared.

"Admiring the centerpiece, are we?"

The voice sent a chill up Rex's spine, smooth as silk but sharpened with intent. He turned to find Miss Whiskers standing beside him, her diamond collar catching the light in a way that mirrored the bone. Her smile was practiced, but her eyes were watchful, calculating every inch of his expression.

"Just taking in the view," Rex replied, keeping his voice casual. "Seems like quite the item to end up here."

"Doesn't it?" Miss Whiskers purred, stepping closer. "It's funny how treasures like this have a way of resurfacing. Almost as though they want to be found."

"Or stolen," Rex said, tilting his head.

Her smile didn't falter. "That depends on the thief."

Rex turned his gaze back to the photograph, his mind spinning. "Anonymous buyer, huh? Strange how something so valuable winds up belonging to no one at all."

Miss Whiskers leaned in, her voice just above a whisper. "You of all hounds should know, Detective. Ownership is rarely about who holds the leash—it's about who pulls it."

Rex studied her, his nose twitching at the faint scent of lavender and catnip that always seemed to follow her. "Speaking of pulling strings, you wouldn't happen to know who put this little gem back on the market, would you?"

Her eyes glimmered, sharp and unreadable. "Why, Detective, if I knew, I'd hardly tell you. After all, a girl must have her secrets."

Before Rex could push further, a voice from the stage interrupted them—Baron Poodle's deep bark. "The auction begins in fifteen minutes. Guests, prepare your bids."

Miss Whiskers straightened, smoothing her gown with a satisfied smile. "It seems I'm needed elsewhere. Enjoy the show, Detective."

She disappeared into the crowd, leaving Rex standing alone in front of the photograph. He stared at the glittering bone in the frame, the whispers of the Cartel and black-market dealings still bouncing around his head. Whoever bought it hadn't just wanted a pretty trinket—they wanted power.

Rex's gut twisted. He didn't know who was holding the leash yet, but someone was pulling hard.

"Time to find out who's holding the other end," Rex muttered, turning his eyes to the auction floor, where the real games were about to begin.

The Kennel Club gala had turned from glitz to trouble faster than Rex Barkley could flick his tail. The moment the word "waiter" got whispered in the wrong ears, he knew his cover had cracked wide open. He saw it in the sudden shift of eyes— a tuxedoed bulldog straightening near the door, a pair of Dobermans exchanging looks, and Bentley Poodle's suspicious gaze narrowing from the auction stage. The air grew heavy, the hum of conversation dipping just slightly as Rex felt the tension coil around him like a leash about to snap.

Time to move, Barkley, his instincts growled.

Rex's nose caught something sharp—panic, sweat, the faint metallic scent of his own nerves—and he turned just in time to see one of the bulldogs nod toward him. The dog's thick paws curled into fists as he pushed away from the wall.

"Hey!" the bulldog barked, his deep voice carrying across the room. "You—where's your pass?"

Rex kept his tray steady, his expression a mask of calm. "Pass?" he replied, glancing over his shoulder as though the accusation wasn't for him. "Sorry, pal, you've got the wrong hound."

"Don't play dumb!" the bulldog snarled, shoving past a table of spaniels. "Stop right there!"

Rex cursed under his breath. He slipped the tray onto a table and spun toward the nearest corridor, his trench coat snapping behind him. *Keep moving*, he thought. *Don't let them box you in.*

"Get him!" another voice shouted, and the sound of pounding paws filled the hall.

Rex pushed through a set of gilded double doors, finding himself in a narrow service hallway. The fluorescent lights buzzed overhead, casting harsh shadows on the cracked tile. Rex's boots thudded in rhythm as he bolted past stacks of crates and wheeled carts, his breath steady despite the adrenaline spiking through him.

"Cut him off!"

The shout came from behind, closer now, as the bulldogs charged after him, heavy footfalls shaking the floor. Rex's eyes darted left and right, searching for an escape route. Ahead, a small storage room door hung slightly ajar. Rex didn't hesitate—he slipped inside and pressed his back to the wall, his ears tuned to the approaching chaos.

The voices grew louder, then stopped just outside.

"Where'd he go?"

"I saw him come this way!"

"Well, he ain't here now. Check the other hall!"

Rex held his breath as the shadows outside shifted, one of the guards lingering just beyond the doorway. Through the crack in the door, Rex could see the bulldog's broad shoulders and twitching ears as he scanned the hallway. A drop of sweat slid down Rex's brow, though his face stayed stone-cold calm.

"Move it!" a Doberman barked. "We'll sweep the east wing."

The bulldog grumbled but turned away, his heavy steps fading into the distance.

Rex exhaled quietly, letting the tension ease just a notch. He counted to five, then carefully cracked the door and slipped back into the hall. The path was clear, for now. His ears twitched as he heard the faint din of the gala growing distant—
good.

He moved quickly, his nose catching another scent now—one that made him stop mid-step. Something sharp and papery. He looked down to see it: a torn scrap, half-hidden under a tipped-over crate.

Rex crouched and scooped it up. The paper was creased and damp around the edges, like someone had crumpled it in a hurry. There, scrawled in thick, hasty lines, were coordinates. His brow furrowed as he read them. He didn't need a map to know where they led.

The docks.

"Figures," Rex muttered, tucking the paper into his coat.

Before he could move again, a sharp bark erupted behind him.

"There he is!"

Rex turned just in time to see one of the bulldogs burst into the hall, followed by another guard. They were charging at full speed, paws pounding the floor like thunder.

No time to think.

Rex bolted, his trench coat streaming behind him as he veered toward a side exit. He slammed through a metal door, spilling into an alley slick with rain and the faint glow of streetlights. The cold air hit him like a slap, but he didn't slow down. Behind him, the guards thundered through the door, their growls echoing off the brick walls.

"There's nowhere to run, hound!"

"Watch me!" Rex shouted back, his boots splashing through puddles as he skidded around a corner.

He cut through the maze of narrow alleys, his nose working overtime to track the cleanest escape route. The guards' voices grew fainter, but Rex didn't stop moving until the sound of pursuit had finally vanished into the distance. Only then did he allow himself to slow, leaning against a graffiti-streaked wall to catch his breath.

Rain streamed off his hat and coat, pooling at his feet as he fished the crumpled scrap of paper from his pocket. He held it up under a flickering streetlamp, the numbers on the page glaring back at him like a dare.

"The docks," Rex muttered, his breath still heavy. "Everything points to the docks."

The smell of fish oil, saltwater, and trouble practically leapt off the page. Whoever was pulling the strings in this mess was counting on him staying one step behind. But Rex wasn't about to let that happen.

He pushed off the wall, straightening his coat with a grimace as the pain in his leg flared again. It didn't matter. He'd taken hits before, and he'd take more before this was done. Someone wanted him out of the game, but they'd underestimated the hound they were dealing with.

"Keep running, you crooks," Rex muttered, shoving the paper back into his coat. "I'll be right on your tail."

The rain fell harder as he limped back into the city's shadows, the docks waiting for him like a dark promise. The coordinates were just a lead, but in Barkington, every lead came with a price. Rex only hoped he'd survive long enough to pay it.

Chapter 6
The Dockside Web

The docks at night had their own soundtrack: the rhythmic lapping of waves against the pylons, the groan of rusted cranes swaying in the breeze, and the low hum of voices muffled by the cavernous echoes of the warehouses. Rex Barkley walked the narrow path between stacks of shipping containers, his boots tapping against the damp concrete. The faint scent of fish oil still clung to the air, though now it mingled with the sharper tang of diesel.

Ahead, the faint glow of a halogen light outlined a cluster of figures. Mittens Malone stood at the center of the group, his sleek black fur catching the light in sharp, polished lines. He was every bit the kingpin Rex remembered—confident, sharp-eyed, and dressed like he belonged in a casino lounge rather than a shipping yard. A trio of muscle surrounded him: a burly Maine Coon, a scrappy Siamese, and a lanky ginger with a scar cutting through one ear. They leaned against the crates like they didn't have a care in the world, but their eyes tracked Rex's every move.

"Well, well," Mittens said, his voice smooth as silk but with an edge sharp enough to cut glass. "If it isn't Rex Barkley, the hound who doesn't know when to quit."

"I don't quit, Mittens," Rex said, stopping just short of the pool of light. "Not when the trail smells this bad."

Mittens chuckled, a low, rumbling sound that didn't quite reach his eyes. "You've got guts showing up here, I'll give you that. Guts and a death wish. Tell me, Rex, what brings you to my little corner of the city tonight?"

"I'm here for answers," Rex replied, his tone steady. "About the bone."

Mittens' ears twitched, and the amusement in his eyes dimmed just slightly. "The bone," he repeated, as though tasting the word. "You're barking up the wrong tree, my friend. That little trinket isn't my concern."

"Cut the act," Rex said, stepping forward. The ginger hissed and straightened, but a quick flick of Mittens' paw kept him in check. "I've followed the trail, Mittens. Fish oil, pawprints, thugs with your stink all over them. It all points back to you."

Mittens tilted his head, his tail flicking lazily. "Thugs, you say? I'd say I'm insulted, but I've got bigger fish to fry. Whatever mess you've sniffed out, it's not my doing."

"Then who's?" Rex shot back, his voice rising. "Because someone wanted that bone bad enough to stage a break-in, leave a trail, and send your goons after me."

The Maine Coon growled low, but Mittens raised a paw again, silencing him. "You're playing a dangerous game, Barkley," Mittens said, his tone soft but menacing. "Poking your nose where it doesn't belong is a good way to lose it."

"Save the threats," Rex replied, crossing his arms. "We both know you're not the kind of cat to get your paws dirty unless there's something in it for you. So what's the play, Mittens? What's so special about that bone?"

For a moment, the only sound was the faint creak of the dock's wooden planks beneath their feet. Then Mittens sighed, a slow, deliberate exhale. "You think you've got it all figured out, don't you?" he said, stepping closer. "You think this is about a bone?"

Rex's ears twitched, catching the shift in Mittens' tone. "Why don't you enlighten me?"

Mittens gave a humorless chuckle, his golden eyes narrowing. "That bone is more than just a shiny trinket, Rex. It's leverage. Power. The kind of thing that makes people do stupid things— like trust the wrong cat."

"Miss Whiskers," Rex said, his voice low. "What's her angle in all this?"

Mittens' expression darkened, and for the first time, Rex saw a flicker of something beneath the surface—anger, hurt, maybe even regret. "Whiskers," Mittens said, almost spitting the name. "You want to know about her? Fine. She's the reason the Cartel's been sniffing around. The reason that bone's gone missing."

"Talk," Rex demanded. "Start from the beginning."

Mittens hesitated, his tail lashing once before he spoke. "Whiskers and I go way back," he said, his voice softer now. "Back when we were both clawing our way out of the gutter. We made a good team—me with the muscle, her with the brains. We built something together, something real."

"So what happened?" Rex asked, his voice cutting through the tension.

"What always happens," Mittens replied bitterly. "Greed. Ambition. She wanted more, and she didn't care who she stepped on to get it. She turned on me, sold me out to the Cartel. I barely made it out alive."

Rex frowned, the pieces starting to click into place. "And now she's back, looking for the bone."

"Not looking," Mittens said, his eyes blazing. "Scheming. She doesn't care about that bone, Rex. She cares about what it represents. She wants control—over me, over the Cartel, over this whole damn city."

"And you're just an innocent bystander?" Rex asked, his tone skeptical.

Mittens smirked, though there was no humor in it. "Innocent? Not by a long shot. But this time, I'm not the one playing dirty."

Rex studied him carefully, his instincts warring with his better judgment. Mittens Malone was a lot of things—a liar, a criminal, a schemer—but he wasn't stupid. If he said Miss

Whiskers was pulling the strings, there was a good chance he was telling the truth.

"You've got a choice to make, Barkley," Mittens said, his voice low and serious. "You keep chasing this bone, you're gonna find yourself in the middle of a war. And trust me, neither side gives a damn about what happens to you."

Rex straightened, his resolve hardening. "I don't back down from a fight, Mittens. You should know that by now."

Mittens sighed, shaking his head. "Then I hope you're ready for what's coming."

As Rex turned to leave, the rain started to fall again, washing away the tension but leaving the weight of Mittens' words heavy in the air. The game was bigger than he'd thought, but Rex wasn't about to fold. Not yet.

The rain tapped a steady rhythm against the corrugated metal roof of the dockside warehouse, its muffled cadence filling the silence after Mittens Malone's revelation. Rex Barkley stood motionless, the low hum of tension between them crackling like static in the humid air. The Rottweiler and his goons kept their distance, though their narrowed eyes and twitching paws suggested they were waiting for a signal from their boss.

"You've got my attention, Mittens," Rex said finally, his voice as steady as his gaze. "You're saying this bone is more than just a flashy chew toy. What's it really worth?"

Mittens smirked, his tail swishing behind him in slow, deliberate arcs. "It's worth more than your life, Barkley. Worth more than mine, too, if we're being honest."

"That's not saying much," Rex quipped, though his tone was edged with curiosity. "Cut the drama. What's the play here? What makes that bone so special?"

Mittens stepped forward, his sharp claws clicking softly against the concrete floor. The light from a single halogen bulb overhead cast his features into sharp relief, his golden eyes gleaming with a dangerous mix of ambition and bitterness. "That bone, Rex, isn't just a family heirloom. It's a key—a symbol of power, leverage, and everything that keeps the Cartel in check."

"A key to what?" Rex pressed, his brow furrowing.

Mittens gestured toward a nearby stack of crates, his claws scratching a line across the wood. "The Cartel has rules, Rex. Alliances. Agreements that keep this city from tearing itself apart. That bone isn't just an ornament—it's proof of ownership, a sign of who holds the real power in this town."

Rex tilted his head, his ears twitching. "You're telling me the Cartel's power struggles come down to a glorified chew toy?"

"Call it whatever you want," Mittens replied, his voice low but sharp. "But the boss who holds that bone doesn't just control the Cartel—they control the flow of power in Barkington. It's not just leverage. It's legitimacy."

"Legitimacy," Rex repeated, his tone laced with skepticism. "Sounds like a load of litter box filler. You really expect me to believe a shiny bone is the cornerstone of your whole operation?"

Mittens' smirk faded, replaced by a flicker of irritation. "Believe what you want, hound, but that bone represents a legacy. It's been in the Cartel's possession for decades, passed down from one boss to the next. Losing it isn't just embarrassing—it's dangerous."

"Dangerous how?" Rex asked, crossing his arms.

Mittens paused, his tail flicking with restrained agitation. "You don't get it, do you? The Cartel isn't just one gang—it's a dozen, all clawing for control. That bone keeps them in line, a reminder that there's one boss at the top. Without it..." He shrugged, his expression dark. "Without it, the whole system collapses. Every two-bit thug in the city will start staking claims, and the blood will flow faster than the rain."

Rex's eyes narrowed as he processed the information. The bone wasn't just a bauble; it was a symbol, a relic of authority that held the fragile balance of power in Barkington together. "So, whoever's got the bone holds the leash on the Cartel," he said slowly. "And without it, your whole empire comes crumbling down."

Mittens met his gaze, his expression unreadable. "Exactly. That's why it's gone missing, Rex. Someone wanted to upset the balance—someone who knew what that bone really meant."

"And you're saying that someone isn't you," Rex said, his tone skeptical.

"If I wanted to start a war, I wouldn't need a damn bone to do it," Mittens shot back, his voice rising. "I built my power with my claws and my wits, not with some shiny heirloom."

"Then who's playing this game?" Rex asked, stepping closer. "Who's pulling the strings?"

Mittens' ears flattened slightly, and for the first time, Rex saw a flicker of doubt in the cat's sharp gaze. "That's the million-dollar question, isn't it? Whoever took the bone knew exactly what they were doing. It's not just about power—it's about chaos."

"Miss Whiskers," Rex said, the name hanging in the air like a loaded gun.

Mittens stiffened, his jaw tightening. "Whiskers is smart, I'll give her that. Too smart. But if she's involved, she's not acting alone. This is bigger than her, Barkley. Bigger than me.

Someone out there wants the Cartel to fall apart, and they're willing to burn the whole city to do it."

Rex studied him carefully, his instincts buzzing with the weight of Mittens' words. The bone wasn't just a piece of jewelry or a relic of nostalgia. It was a weapon, and someone was wielding it to unravel the city's delicate balance.

"You've got a lot of enemies, Mittens," Rex said finally. "What makes you so sure you're not the target?"

Mittens let out a bitter laugh, his sharp teeth glinting in the dim light. "I'm always the target, Rex. But this? This isn't about taking me down. It's about taking us all down."

The rain grew louder, a relentless drumbeat against the metal roof. Rex's mind churned with questions, but one thing was clear: the bone was the key to everything, and the stakes were higher than he'd imagined.

"You've given me a lot to think about," Rex said, his tone guarded. "But I've got one more question."

"Make it quick," Mittens replied, his tail flicking impatiently.

"If this bone is so damn important," Rex said, his voice cutting through the rain, "why didn't you guard it better?"

Mittens' eyes flashed, his claws flexing against the concrete. "I didn't lose it, Barkley. But I'll be the one to get it back."

"Not if I find it first," Rex replied, turning toward the warehouse door. "And when I do, you'll be the second to know."

As Rex stepped back into the storm, Mittens' words echoed in his mind. The bone wasn't just leverage—it was a fuse, and someone had already lit the match.

The rain hadn't let up, turning the docks into a shimmering maze of puddles and slick concrete. Rex Barkley stood across from Mittens Malone, the air between them heavy with unspoken tension. The faint hum of dock machinery in the background did little to mask the sharp undertone in Mittens' voice as he spoke, his tail flicking with restrained agitation.

"Barkley," Mittens said, his golden eyes narrowing. "This isn't your fight. Walk away while you still can."

Rex tilted his head, water dripping from the brim of his hat. "You don't strike me as the altruistic type, Mittens. Why the sudden concern for my well-being?"

"It's not concern," Mittens replied, his tone clipped. "It's practicality. You've got a nose for trouble, but you don't know how deep this goes. You keep digging, and you're not gonna like what you find."

"I've already found plenty," Rex said, crossing his arms. "Miss Whiskers, the bone, the Cartel—it's all connected. You just don't want me finding out how."

Mittens stepped closer, his claws clicking softly against the wet concrete. His voice dropped to a low growl, the kind that sent shivers down spines. "You think you're chasing the truth, but you're just chasing your own tail. Whiskers has you wrapped around her little paw, and you don't even see it."

Rex raised an eyebrow, his expression unreadable. "Is that so?"

"She's playing you, Barkley," Mittens said, his voice rising slightly. "That bone isn't just a trophy for her—it's leverage. And once she gets what she wants, she'll toss you aside like yesterday's litter."

Rex studied him carefully, his instincts buzzing. "Funny, you're awfully worried about her using me. Almost sounds like you're still sore about getting played yourself."

Mittens' ears flattened, and for a moment, the calm facade cracked. "Whiskers and I have history," he said, his voice tight. "She's good at making you believe she's on your side until she's not. Trust me, Rex. You don't want to end up like me."

"I'll take my chances," Rex said, his tone steady. "Now, unless you've got something useful to add, I've got a bone to catch."

Mittens let out a bitter laugh, shaking his head. "You're a stubborn mutt, I'll give you that. Just remember—you were warned."

Rex tipped his hat, his eyes never leaving Mittens' sharp gaze. "Appreciate the advice. Try not to miss me when I prove you wrong."

As Rex turned to leave, the rain picked up, its steady rhythm punctuated by the occasional clang of metal against metal. The thugs surrounding Mittens exchanged glances but didn't move to stop him. It wasn't a show of respect—it was a show of calculation. They knew as well as Rex did that this wasn't over.

He walked down the long stretch of the docks, the smell of saltwater and diesel thick in the air. The conversation with Mittens gnawed at him, but it wasn't enough to make him stop. He'd dealt with liars, schemers, and worse before. Whatever Miss Whiskers was hiding, he'd find out soon enough.

Rex's boots splashed through a shallow puddle, and he stopped mid-stride. Something caught his eye—a faint carving etched into the side of a nearby shipping crate. He stepped closer, crouching to get a better look. The rain blurred the edges of the mark, but the shape was unmistakable: a glyph, identical to the one he'd seen at Miss Whiskers' penthouse.

"Not just a coincidence," Rex muttered to himself, running his paw over the damp surface. The carving was deliberate, its lines sharp and precise. This wasn't some random scrawl left by a bored dock worker—it was a message, just like before.

He straightened, his sharp eyes scanning the area. The glyph wasn't fresh, but it was recent enough to matter. Whoever had left it here had done so for a reason, and Rex was certain it tied back to the staged robbery. The bone, the Cartel, the penthouse—it was all part of a larger puzzle, and this glyph was another piece.

A faint sound made Rex turn his head. In the distance, a shadow moved between two stacks of crates, barely visible through the rain. He couldn't make out the figure, but he didn't need to. Someone was watching him, and they weren't being subtle about it.

"Guess I'm not the only one chasing leads tonight," Rex said under his breath.

He adjusted his hat, his jaw tightening. The docks were a labyrinth of hiding spots and dead ends, and whoever was lurking out there had the advantage of knowing the terrain. Rex wasn't about to play cat and mouse—especially not with his ribs still aching from the earlier ambush.

He turned back to the glyph, pulling his notebook from his coat pocket. With quick, practiced movements, he sketched the carving, noting its exact location. If this symbol kept showing up, it meant something. And Rex intended to find out what.

As he closed the notebook and slid it back into his pocket, the rain eased slightly, the storm retreating to a steady drizzle. The docks were quiet again, the sounds of activity fading into the background. But the weight of the evening lingered, heavy and oppressive.

Rex straightened, his resolve hardening. The warnings from Mittens, the glyph, the lurking shadow—they were all pieces of a bigger game. And Rex Barkley wasn't the kind of dog to fold under pressure.

With one last glance at the glyph, he turned and walked away, the sound of his boots lost in the rain. The path ahead was murky, but Rex had never needed clear skies to follow a trail. Whatever game Miss Whiskers and the Cartel were playing, he was all in now.

Chapter 7
Faint Whiffs of Betrayal

Rex Barkley stood at the base of Miss Whiskers' towering penthouse, the rain pattering faintly against his coat as he stared up at the monolith of glass and marble. The lights glowed soft and golden through the tall windows, too warm and perfect for a place that had been the setting of so much trouble. Rex wasn't a fool; any invitation from Miss Whiskers carried more strings than a puppeteer's stage.

With a grunt, he pushed through the polished glass doors and rode the elevator in silence. The faint hum of the machinery gave him time to think. Frankie's words were still fresh in his ears—whispers of the bone's power, the tangled threads of the Alley Cartel, and a game that stretched far beyond anyone's reach. At the center of it all sat Miss Whiskers, poised and polished, with claws that scratched just deep enough to leave scars.

When the elevator opened, Rex was greeted by the faint, familiar scent of lavender. The penthouse was as pristine as ever—polished marble floors, spotless velvet furniture, the faint hum of city life muffled by the thick glass walls. But there was something else in the air tonight—something he couldn't quite name. It wasn't just lavender anymore. It was uncertainty.

"Detective Barkley."

Her voice drifted in softly from the far end of the room. Miss Whiskers was seated on one of the white leather couches, a glass of something amber-colored resting delicately in her paw. The robe she wore was silk, the same shade of cream as her fur, and her diamond collar glimmered faintly under the chandelier's light.

"You're a hard hound to pin down," she said, her gaze lifting to meet his. "I was beginning to think you'd gotten lost."

"I don't get lost," Rex said gruffly, stepping into the room. "I just don't always like where the trail takes me."

He moved toward the couch, his boots muffled against the thick carpet. Miss Whiskers gestured toward the chair across from her, a subtle invitation that felt more like a test. Rex didn't sit.

"Something on your mind, Detective?" she asked, her voice smooth as silk but edged with a faint tremor, like a tightrope stretched too far.

"Plenty," Rex replied, his eyes narrowing. "I've been talking to some friends of yours. Word is you and the Alley Cartel have history."

Miss Whiskers' paw stilled on her glass. She didn't flinch, but her eyes flickered—just a spark, just enough to show she hadn't expected him to dive straight into the truth. "And what did they say?"

"That depends," Rex said, his voice steady. "You gonna tell me they're lying?"

Miss Whiskers exhaled softly, a sound that wasn't quite a sigh but wasn't far off. She set the glass down gently on the table, the faint clink echoing in the otherwise quiet room. When she looked back at Rex, there was no sly smile, no veil of charm. Just a weariness that seemed out of place on someone who always appeared untouchable.

"I won't lie to you, Detective," she said finally, her voice low. "Yes, I knew the Alley Cartel. I ran with them once—long ago."

Rex's brow furrowed, his nose twitching. "You don't strike me as the type who runs anywhere, Miss Whiskers. You make others do the running for you."

Her mouth curled faintly, though it didn't reach her eyes. "Back then, I wasn't the Miss Whiskers you see before you. I was young, reckless. I thought alliances could be bought like diamonds. I was wrong."

Rex folded his arms across his chest, watching her carefully. "Why'd you leave?"

She leaned back against the couch, her gaze drifting toward the window where the city lights sprawled out like constellations. "Because the Cartel doesn't let anyone leave clean, Detective. When you're in, you're in for life. I saw what they were becoming—the power they wanted, the lengths they'd go to claim it. I knew if I stayed, I'd lose myself."

"And yet," Rex said, his voice cutting through the quiet, "here we are, chasing ghosts from that same past."

Miss Whiskers turned back to him, something sharp and unreadable flickering behind her blue eyes. "You think I wanted this? That I asked for the bone to resurface and drag me back into the shadows? I left that life. I *built* this life. But the past doesn't let go, Detective, no matter how far you try to run."

Rex studied her carefully, his instincts prickling. The vulnerability in her voice was real—he could smell it, almost taste it—but something still didn't add up. She was too careful, too practiced. Even now, when she let her guard down, she only let it slip just enough.

"You're leaving something out," Rex said after a beat, his voice low. "You always leave something out."

Miss Whiskers' eyes hardened slightly, the faintest flicker of steel returning to her voice. "Maybe I am. But tell me, Detective—can you blame me? You walk into a room like a storm cloud with ears. How can I trust you when you barely trust yourself?"

Rex didn't answer right away. The city outside seemed to stretch endlessly, the sound of distant sirens barely audible through the thick glass. He shifted his weight slightly, his gaze never leaving hers.

"I don't need you to trust me," he said finally, his tone gravelly. "I just need the truth. All of it."

Miss Whiskers' expression softened again, though the guarded look in her eyes didn't vanish completely. "I've told you what matters, Detective. I left the Cartel to start fresh. Whatever's happening now… I didn't start it."

Rex stared at her for a long moment, his gut telling him two things at once—that she was telling the truth, and that she was still hiding the part that mattered most. He turned slightly, adjusting his hat as he glanced back toward the door.

"This life you built, Miss Whiskers," Rex said, his voice quiet but firm, "it's cracking. And sooner or later, the truth's gonna pour through."

Miss Whiskers didn't respond. She just watched him as he turned and walked toward the elevator, her glass of amber liquid sitting untouched on the table.

As the elevator doors slid shut behind him, Rex exhaled slowly, his mind churning. She was hiding something—she always was—but there was truth in her words. The Cartel, the bone, and Miss Whiskers' past were tangled together tighter than a noose. And Rex Barkley wasn't the type to walk away before he loosened every knot.

Rex Barkley stepped off the elevator into the cold night air, the city lights glittering like shattered glass in the distance. The rain had started up again—light and steady, just enough to turn the streets slick and dangerous. He pulled his collar tight against the wind and limped toward his office. His mind churned, the pieces of the case sliding into place like jagged puzzle pieces that didn't quite fit. Miss Whiskers' confession gnawed at him—half-truths mixed with silk-covered lies. She'd left the Cartel, sure, but something told him she'd never really escaped.

As Rex rounded the corner onto Hound Street, he noticed a shadow leaning against the brick wall just outside his office building. The glow of a cigar flared in the dark, followed by a thin stream of smoke curling up into the rain. Rex slowed his pace, his boots echoing against the pavement. His nose twitched as the scent hit him—tobacco, musk, and the faint undercurrent of authority.

"Commissioner Bowser," Rex said, his voice gravelly. "Didn't expect to see you waiting outside my door. You lost, or did you miss me?"

The figure shifted, stepping out of the shadows and into the faint light spilling from the lamppost above. **Commissioner Bowser** was a mastiff with a build like a brick wall and a face that looked carved from stone. His trench coat, darker than the night around him, flared slightly in the wind as he exhaled another cloud of smoke. His eyes—cold, unreadable—settled on Rex with a weight that could bury a lesser hound.

"You're in over your head, Barkley," Bowser growled, his voice as heavy as gravel rolling downhill. "Figured I'd save you the trouble of finding that out the hard way."

Rex stopped a few feet away, folding his arms across his chest. "Appreciate the concern, Commissioner, but I don't need a babysitter."

Bowser let out a short, humorless laugh. "This ain't concern. It's a warning." He jabbed the lit end of his cigar in Rex's direction, the ember glowing like an angry eye. "You've been kicking up dust where it don't belong—sticking your nose in places even the rats are smart enough to avoid."

"That so?" Rex tilted his head, his gaze never leaving Bowser's. "Funny, I thought uncovering the truth was what you paid me for."

"That was before you started barking up the wrong trees," Bowser shot back, his tone hardening. "You're not just messing with alley cats anymore, Barkley. The Kennel Club, the Alley Cartel—they don't like loose ends."

Rex's eyes narrowed. "Loose ends like me, you mean."

Bowser took a long drag of his cigar, the ember flaring brighter before he exhaled slowly, letting the smoke curl lazily into the air. "Yeah, like you. You think this is just another case—a missing trinket, a jealous rival? It's bigger than that. It's bigger than you."

"Maybe," Rex said evenly. "But that's never stopped me before."

Bowser stepped forward, closing the space between them. The mastiff's bulk loomed, his shadow stretching long across the rain-slick pavement. "This city's built on a foundation of deals, Barkley—ones you don't see and don't ask about. The bone, the Diamond Key… it's a symbol, sure, but you don't get it. It's a lever, and someone's about to use it to flip this whole city upside down."

Rex didn't flinch. "You sound like you've got a stake in this, Commissioner. Care to share what side of the line you're on?"

Bowser's jaw tightened, the faintest flicker of something—anger, or maybe guilt—crossing his face. "I'm on the side that keeps the peace. You stir this up, Barkley, and it's gonna spill over into the streets. The Kennel Club's got claws in the city's pockets, and the Alley Cartel's got their teeth in everything else. You keep poking at this, and all you're gonna find is blood."

"Blood's already been spilled," Rex replied, his voice sharp as broken glass. "You just want me to look the other way."

Bowser's gaze hardened. "You're playing hero in a game that doesn't need one. You think you can fix this city? You can't. No one can." He flicked the ash from his cigar and took another step closer, his voice dropping to a growl. "Let it go, Barkley. Before it buries you."

Rex stared up at him, unblinking. The rain dripped steadily from the brim of his hat, the city's hum filling the silence between them. "Letting things go ain't my style, Bowser. You know that."

Bowser shook his head slowly, a deep rumble in his chest that might've been a laugh—or a warning. "Stubborn mutt. Don't say I didn't try." He turned then, his broad frame disappearing back into the dark, the glow of his cigar lingering for a moment before it, too, vanished.

Rex watched him go, his paws curled into fists at his sides. The Commissioner's words weighed heavy in the night air, but Rex wasn't the kind of hound to take warnings at face value. If Bowser was trying to scare him off, it meant he was close—too close to something someone didn't want found.

Rex turned back toward his office, his boots splashing through shallow puddles as he muttered to himself, "If the Kennel Club and the Cartel don't like loose ends, they're gonna hate me."

The door clicked shut behind him as he stepped inside, the quiet of his office pressing down like the calm before a storm. He pulled off his coat, hung it on the hook, and stared out the window at the sprawling city below. Somewhere out there, the bone, the Diamond Key, and the truth were waiting for him.

And no warning, no commissioner, and no cartel was going to stop him from sniffing it out.

Rex Barkley sat at his battered desk, the steady tap of rain against the window punctuating the silence. The dim light from his desk lamp cast deep shadows across the room, a reflection of the thoughts swirling in his head. His trench coat hung on the door like a silent sentry, still dripping from the night's downpour. A half-empty glass of whiskey sat next to his paw, the amber liquid catching the light. He hadn't touched it in minutes. He was too busy staring at the mess on his desk.

Files, scraps of paper, and notes were strewn in every direction, a web of leads and lies he'd been chasing since the moment Miss Whiskers stepped through his door. At the center of it all sat the torn scrap of coordinates he'd wrestled out of the chaos earlier that night. It pointed to the docks, sure, but there was something about it—something gnawing at the edges of his gut.

How deep does this go?

Bowser's words rang in his ears, low and gruff, like the growl of a storm that hadn't yet hit. *"The Kennel Club and the Alley Cartel don't like loose ends."* It was a warning, clear as day, but Rex had seen enough to know when someone was holding back. Bowser wasn't just trying to keep the peace—he was trying to bury something. The only question was *what*.

Rex leaned back in his chair, rubbing his tired eyes with the heel of his paw. "Compromised," he muttered under his breath. "Bowser's got his tail caught in something. Just a matter of who's holding the leash."

But Bowser wasn't the only one clawing at his mind. Rex couldn't shake the look Miss Whiskers had given him earlier that night—the way her voice softened, the way she wore vulnerability like a veil, showing just enough to draw him in. She was smart. Too smart. A cat like her didn't let her guard down unless she wanted you to think she had.

"Is she playing me?" Rex asked the empty room, his voice low and gravelly. He wasn't used to asking questions like that—not out loud, not to himself—but the weight of doubt hung heavy around his neck. He'd trusted his nose his whole life, followed scents through shadows and schemes. But now the air smelled like lies, and he was starting to wonder if he could tell which ones were fresh.

The creak of the old radiator filled the silence, and Rex glanced at the glass of whiskey, finally reaching for it. He let the liquid settle on his tongue before swallowing, letting the burn drag him back into focus.

Stay sharp, Barkley. Doubt'll kill you faster than a knife in the dark.

He flipped through the papers again, trying to pull the threads tighter. Miss Whiskers and her past with the Cartel. The bone— no, the *Diamond Key*. Bowser and his warning about powers bigger than Rex could imagine. It all connected. Somehow.

The question was: *who was pulling the strings?*

He thought back to Miss Whiskers' penthouse—her practiced words, her carefully curated vulnerability.

"I left the Cartel to start fresh," she'd said. *"Whatever's happening now... I didn't start it."*

She'd sounded convincing. But cats like Miss Whiskers didn't make mistakes. Everything was calculated. And Rex couldn't shake the feeling that he was a piece on her board, moving exactly where she wanted him.

His eyes narrowed at the thought. "You came to me for a reason, didn't you?" he muttered. "I'm just the hound you need to take the fall when this thing explodes."

He pushed back from his desk, his chair groaning in protest as he stood. His reflection stared back at him from the rain-streaked window—a tired bloodhound with too many bruises and too few answers. He leaned forward, his paws braced against the sill as he stared out at the dark city below.

Barkington stretched endlessly before him, a maze of shadows and glinting lights, where secrets pooled in every crack and corner. Somewhere out there, someone had the answers. And Rex was starting to think he didn't want to know all of them.

You're in too deep.

The thought whispered in the back of his mind, the way a voice does when it's saying something you don't want to hear. But Rex pushed it aside. He'd never been one to turn back, no matter how deep the water got.

Behind him, the door creaked.

Rex turned sharply, his instincts firing on all cylinders. His paw drifted to the edge of his desk where he kept a small revolver, but the room was empty save for the faint draft seeping through the window's cracks.

He let out a slow breath. "Paranoid now, huh, Barkley?" he muttered, shaking his head. "They're already under your skin."

He turned back to the desk, his gaze falling on the mess of papers. Bowser's warning, Miss Whiskers' lies, Frankie's half-spilled truths. It was all starting to fray the edges of his trust—trust in the case, trust in his instincts, and maybe trust in himself.

"Doesn't matter," he said quietly to the room. "I'll get to the bottom of this. One way or another."

The rain outside picked up again, drumming against the window like a thousand tiny warnings. Rex poured another glass of whiskey and sank back into his chair, his gaze locked on the map spread across his desk. The docks still waited for him, the coordinates burning a hole in his pocket.

But before he got there, Rex knew one thing: he needed to figure out who was lying to him first—Miss Whiskers, Bowser, or both.

And when he did, someone was going to pay for it.

Chapter 8
A City on Edge

The dim glow of a flickering streetlamp cast long, jittery shadows across the damp alley where Rex Barkley leaned against a graffiti-streaked wall. The air was thick with the smell of wet asphalt and stale garbage, but Rex barely noticed. His sharp eyes were locked on the jittery Chihuahua in front of him, Sniffles McGruff, who was fidgeting with the brim of his oversized trench coat.

"Sniffles," Rex began, his tone measured but firm. "I don't have time to play games. You're going to tell me what you know about the Cartel, or we're going to have a problem."

Sniffles wrung his paws, his oversized coat almost swallowing his tiny frame as he shuffled nervously. "Rex, buddy, pal—I don't know anything worth knowing. I'm just a little guy trying to keep his nose clean, you know?"

"Clean?" Rex snorted, stepping closer. His towering presence made Sniffles shrink back against the wall. "I can smell the Cartel's stink on you from here. You've been hanging around their edges, sniffing for scraps. Now talk."

"Okay, okay!" Sniffles squeaked, holding up his paws defensively. "I might've heard a thing or two. But you gotta understand, Rex—those cats don't mess around. If they even think I'm talking to you, I'm finished. They'll string me up like yesterday's laundry."

"Keep stalling, and you'll be finished sooner," Rex said flatly, crossing his arms. "Now, what's the Cartel planning? Start with the docks."

Sniffles hesitated, his ears twitching nervously. "Fine," he muttered, his voice barely above a whisper. "The docks are just a staging ground. They've been moving shipments in and out for weeks—fish oil crates, mostly. But it's not just fish oil, Rex. There's something else mixed in, something they're keeping real quiet."

"What kind of something?" Rex pressed, his eyes narrowing.

"I don't know!" Sniffles squeaked again, his tail curling around one leg. "Honest, I don't. But I've seen the way they guard those crates—like they're full of gold or something."

Rex leaned in, his voice dropping to a dangerous whisper. "And the bone? Does it tie into the shipments?"

Sniffles' eyes darted around, as though he expected the Cartel's enforcers to materialize out of the shadows. "Maybe," he said after a long pause. "Word is, the bone's more than just a shiny bauble. It's leverage—something big enough to put a target on anyone who holds it. That's why everyone's so jumpy. They're all waiting to see who's dumb enough to make the first move."

"And Mittens?" Rex asked. "Where does he fit into all this?"

Sniffles hesitated again, visibly weighing his options. Finally, he sighed. "Mittens is stuck in the middle. The Cartel doesn't trust him, and Whiskers is outmaneuvering him at every turn. He's running scared, Rex. He doesn't know who to fight or who to run from."

Rex tilted his head, his instincts buzzing. "And Whiskers? What's her endgame?"

Sniffles gulped, his wide eyes darting back to Rex's face. "She wants the Cartel to fall apart," he whispered. "She's been sowing chaos, turning their allies against each other. The bone's just her way of lighting the fuse."

Rex took a step back, his mind racing as the pieces began to fall into place. "So, the bone's a power play. Whoever controls it controls the Cartel, and Whiskers is using it to burn everything down."

"Exactly," Sniffles said, nodding furiously. "But that means everyone's on edge, Rex. You're walking into a war zone, and trust me—you don't want to be caught in the crossfire."

"I'm already in it," Rex said, adjusting his hat. "Now tell me where I can find the next shipment."

Sniffles hesitated, his tail twitching. "You're not gonna like it, Rex."

"Try me."

"The north docks," Sniffles said reluctantly. "They've got a shipment coming in tomorrow night. That's where they'll be moving the big stuff. But Rex, listen to me—don't do this. You think the thugs in the alley were bad? The ones guarding those crates won't stop at a few bruises."

Rex's lips curled into a faint smirk. "I'll take my chances."

Sniffles sighed, his small shoulders slumping. "Suit yourself, but don't say I didn't warn you."

Rex turned to leave, his boots splashing through the shallow puddles as he walked away. "Stay out of trouble, Sniffles," he called over his shoulder. "And if you hear anything else, you know where to find me."

Sniffles muttered something under his breath, but Rex didn't stick around to hear it. The pieces were starting to come together, but the picture they formed was darker than he'd expected. The Cartel, Whiskers, Mittens, and the bone—it was all part of a bigger game, one that had already claimed too many players.

As he disappeared into the night, the faint sound of Sniffles scurrying away reached his ears, but Rex didn't look back. The north docks were waiting, and so was the next move in a game he couldn't afford to lose.

The rain had eased into a soft drizzle, a rare moment of calm in Barkington's ever-turbulent night. Rex Barkley stood under the awning of a shuttered deli, his back to the flickering neon sign above the door. The dim streetlights reflected off the wet pavement, casting shifting shadows that danced in time with Rex's thoughts. His notebook was open in his hand, the damp pages smudged but legible, each line of hastily scrawled notes connecting the dots that Sniffles had just provided.

"Fish oil shipments," Rex muttered to himself, tapping his pencil against the page. "Guarded like Fort Knox. The bone's tied to leverage, Cartel control, and Whiskers stirring the pot."

The glyphs were the thread that kept tugging at his mind. They weren't just marks left for show—they were deliberate, each one pointing to something bigger. He flipped back to his earlier sketches, comparing the glyph he'd seen at the penthouse with the one near the docks. The symbols weren't identical, but they shared a sharp angularity, a distinct design that couldn't be random.

"Messages," he murmured, his brow furrowing. "Breadcrumbs leading to something bigger."

The pieces didn't just fit—they clanged together like an alarm. Miss Whiskers' staged robbery hadn't been about the bone itself, not entirely. It had been about setting a chain of events into motion, one that painted the Cartel as the villains while leaving her free to manipulate the chaos from the sidelines.

But why? Rex frowned, staring at the page. What did Whiskers gain from dismantling the Cartel? Power, sure—control of Barkington's underworld was a tempting prize for anyone ambitious enough to play the game. But it felt deeper than that.

Personal, even. Something about the way Mittens had spoken of her rang in Rex's mind.

"She's good at making you believe she's on your side," Mittens had said, his voice bitter with the weight of history. Whiskers didn't just play the game—she played people.

Rex tucked the notebook into his pocket, his sharp eyes scanning the empty street. The scent of fish oil still clung faintly to the air, a reminder of the docks and the shipments Sniffles had mentioned. The north docks, Sniffles had said, where the big moves happened. That was where the Cartel would be tomorrow night, guarding their precious cargo like it held the keys to the city.

He pulled his hat lower against the drizzle and started walking, his boots splashing softly against the wet pavement. The rhythmic sound steadied him, grounding his swirling thoughts as he turned the information over in his mind.

The robbery had been staged—of that, Rex was certain. The pristine pawprints, the precise shattering of glass, the glyph carved into the floor—it had all been too neat, too deliberate. Whiskers had wanted him to follow the trail, and she'd made sure it was easy enough to find.

But the question that gnawed at him now was why she'd needed him. If Whiskers was as smart as everyone said—and Rex had no doubt she was—then why involve a third party at all? Why not manipulate the Cartel directly or let the bone disappear quietly?

Unless, Rex realized, she wanted someone else to take the fall.

His jaw tightened, the weight of the revelation settling on his shoulders. Whiskers wasn't just playing a dangerous game—she was stacking the deck. The Cartel was her scapegoat, the bone her excuse to draw Rex deeper into the web. And somewhere in the chaos, Whiskers was poised to emerge on top, free of suspicion and with Barkington's criminal underworld at her feet.

A soft rustle to his left snapped Rex out of his thoughts. He turned sharply, his hand instinctively reaching for the edge of his coat where his flashlight rested. A figure emerged from the shadows, their movements slow and deliberate.

"Relax, Barkley," the figure said, their voice low but unmistakably familiar. It was Sniffles, his trench coat soaked and clinging awkwardly to his wiry frame. "I'm not here to spook you."

"You've got a bad habit of showing up where you don't belong, Sniffles," Rex said, though his tone lacked its usual bite.

Sniffles shuffled closer, his tail twitching nervously. "Look, I was thinking about what I told you earlier. The north docks— they're not just moving shipments out. They're bringing something in, too."

"What kind of something?" Rex asked, his eyes narrowing.

Sniffles hesitated, his ears flattening. "I don't know for sure, but it's big. Whatever it is, they've got every goon in the Cartel on edge. I heard one of them mention 'the delivery,' like it's something they've been waiting on for weeks."

Rex's mind raced, the implications piling on top of his already heavy suspicions. "A delivery," he repeated. "And they didn't say what it was?"

"No," Sniffles said, shaking his head. "But I got the feeling it's tied to the bone. Everything is."

Rex nodded slowly, the final threads of his theory pulling tight. Whiskers had staged the robbery to set the Cartel in motion, to force them into a position where they couldn't afford mistakes. The bone wasn't just leverage—it was bait. And whatever this delivery was, it was the Cartel's next move in a game they didn't realize they were already losing.

"Good work, Sniffles," Rex said, his tone almost begrudging. "Stay low, and keep your ears open. I'll handle the rest."

Sniffles blinked, a mix of relief and confusion washing over his face. "You sure about this, Rex? You're walking into a hornet's nest."

"I've done worse," Rex replied, adjusting his hat. "And if I don't figure this out, nobody will."

As Rex turned and walked into the drizzle, the faint scent of fish oil tugged at his nose once more. The threads were tied, but the knot wasn't secure. Not yet.

The rain fell in uneven patterns now, a whisper one moment, a torrent the next, as if the skies above Barkington couldn't decide on their mood. Rex Barkley adjusted his hat, the brim low enough to shield his sharp eyes from the drizzle but not so low that it hampered his view of the street ahead. His boots struck the pavement with deliberate steps, but his ears were tuned to the faintest sound behind him—the kind of sounds that didn't belong.

A scuff against wet asphalt. The faint splash of hurried footsteps.

Rex's nose twitched. Whoever was tailing him wasn't new to this game, but they weren't perfect either. A faint scent hung in the damp air, something sharper than the usual rain-soaked city grime. It wasn't fish oil this time—something more metallic, tinged with a musk that set his instincts alight.

He didn't break stride, didn't turn his head. Showing his pursuer he was onto them would only push them deeper into the shadows. Instead, Rex slowed slightly, his steps casual as he approached the mouth of an alley. The dim glow of a broken streetlamp cast long, jagged shadows across the narrow space. He stepped inside, his movements deliberate, and waited.

The city's hum filled the silence—distant machinery, the occasional blare of a car horn—but beneath it was a rhythm Rex knew too well. Footsteps, now slowing, hesitant. His pursuer was close. Too close.

Rex shifted his weight, positioning himself just out of the alley's light, and waited until the figure came into view—a blur of movement at the corner of his vision. Then, with the precision of a spring-loaded trap, he lunged.

The figure yelped, a muffled sound of surprise as Rex grabbed their coat and slammed them against the damp brick wall. His flashlight snapped to life, illuminating a scrappy tabby whose wide eyes reflected equal parts fear and fury.

"Let me guess," Rex said, his voice low and gravelly. "You're not here to sell me cookies."

"Get off me, Barkley!" the tabby spat, squirming against Rex's iron grip. "You've got no idea what you're messing with!"

Rex tightened his hold, his eyes narrowing. "Oh, I've got a pretty good idea. You've been following me since the deli. Start talking, or you'll be explaining yourself to the precinct."

The tabby hissed, his claws swiping at the air but finding no purchase. "You think you're so smart," he sneered. "You think you can walk into this mess and come out clean? You're in over your head, hound."

"Try me," Rex shot back, his tone sharp as a whip. "Who sent you? Mittens? Whiskers? Or are you freelancing?"

The tabby's defiance flickered, replaced by something darker—fear. "It doesn't matter who sent me," he said, his voice dropping to a whisper. "You're poking the wrong nests. The Cartel doesn't care about you, Barkley, but keep digging and they will."

Rex leaned in, his flashlight catching the faint glint of a collar tag beneath the tabby's soaked coat. He recognized the mark—a subtle engraving of the same glyph he'd found near the docks. "Looks like you're more than just a hired tail," Rex said, yanking the tag into view. "What does this mean? Why does it keep showing up?"

The tabby snarled, wrenching himself free with a surprising burst of strength. He staggered back, his breathing ragged but defiant. "You don't get it, do you? The glyph isn't for you—it's for them. It's a message, and you're not meant to understand it."

"Then explain it to me," Rex growled, advancing a step.

But the tabby wasn't sticking around. With a sharp turn, he bolted down the alley, his lean frame slipping through the narrow gaps between crates and debris like water through a sieve. Rex cursed under his breath and gave chase, his boots pounding against the slick ground.

The tabby was fast, his lithe body darting through the winding maze of alleys with practiced ease. Rex kept his focus, his eyes locked on the flicker of movement ahead. The rain blurred the edges of his vision, but he pressed on, driven by the nagging sense that this cat was holding onto answers he couldn't afford to lose.

They burst out onto a side street, the tabby skidding to a halt as a delivery truck rumbled past, its headlights cutting through the gloom. Rex closed the gap, his paw outstretched to grab his quarry, but the tabby twisted at the last moment, darting into another alley.

"Damn it," Rex muttered, his pace quickening. He rounded the corner, only to find the alley empty. His eyes darted to the shadows, searching for any sign of movement, but there was nothing—just the steady drip of water from an overhang and the faint echo of his own breath.

He stood there for a moment, his chest heaving as he scanned the area. The tabby was gone, slipped through the cracks like so many others in this city. But the encounter had left more than frustration—it had left questions.

Rex reached into his pocket, pulling out the tag he'd managed to snatch in the scuffle. The glyph stared back at him, its sharp lines etched into the metal like a challenge. The tabby's words echoed in his mind: *'It's a message, and you're not meant to understand it.'*

"Not yet," Rex muttered, slipping the tag back into his coat. "But I will."

As he stepped back into the rain, the faint scent of fish oil tugged at his nose again, mixing with the sharper tang of adrenaline and mystery. The city had plenty of shadows, but Rex was starting to see the threads that connected them. And he wasn't about to stop pulling.

Chapter 9
Threads of Deception

The rain had stopped by the time Rex Barkley reached Miss Whiskers' penthouse. The city lights glistened on the wet streets below, casting an eerie glow against the polished glass facade of her building. Rex adjusted his hat, his coat still damp from the night's chase, and squared his shoulders. He wasn't here for pleasantries. Miss Whiskers had answers, and Rex wasn't leaving until he had them.

The elevator ride up was silent, save for the faint hum of the motor. Each ding of a passing floor felt heavier than the last, the weight of the night pressing against him. When the doors finally slid open, Rex stepped into the opulent foyer, his sharp eyes scanning the room. Miss Whiskers was seated by the grand window, her silhouette framed by the city skyline. She didn't turn as he approached, but her tail swished lazily, a subtle acknowledgment of his presence.

"Detective Barkley," she purred, her voice smooth and composed. "I didn't expect to see you again so soon. Has the city finally run out of mysteries for you to solve?"

"Not quite," Rex replied, his tone cool as he approached. "But it seems all my mysteries keep leading back to you."

She finally turned, her blue eyes gleaming with a mixture of amusement and challenge. "I'll take that as a compliment."

"Don't," Rex said flatly, pulling a chair closer and sitting down. "We need to talk."

Miss Whiskers arched a brow, her expression one of mild curiosity. "About?"

"About the robbery," Rex said, leaning forward. "And about Mittens."

At the mention of Mittens, her tail stilled for the briefest moment before resuming its languid swish. "Mittens," she echoed, her voice as steady as ever. "What about him?"

"You tell me," Rex said, his gaze sharp. "He seems to think you've got a knack for playing people. Says you've been pulling strings behind the scenes, turning the Cartel into your personal chessboard."

Miss Whiskers smiled faintly, though it didn't reach her eyes. "Mittens always did have a flair for dramatics. But then, you already know that, don't you?"

"Save the deflection," Rex said, his voice edged with steel. "You wanted me on this case, Whiskers. You staged the robbery, left a trail, and practically handed me the Cartel's scent on a silver platter. So what's the endgame? What do you really want?"

Miss Whiskers regarded him for a long moment, her expression unreadable. Then, with deliberate grace, she rose from her chair and walked to the window, her gaze drifting over the glittering city below. "You're right, Detective," she said finally. "I did stage the robbery. But not for the reasons you think."

"Enlighten me," Rex said, his voice cautious.

She turned back to him, her blue eyes colder now. "The Cartel is a cancer, Detective. It's been festering in this city for years, feeding off fear and corruption. And Mittens? He's just another symptom. I'm not playing a game—I'm trying to end one."

Rex frowned, his mind working to piece together her words. "End one? By dragging me into it? By turning the Cartel against itself?"

Miss Whiskers stepped closer, her composure cracking just enough to reveal a sliver of frustration. "The Cartel's power lies in its unity, Detective. As long as they believe in their hierarchy, they're untouchable. But take away their symbol—their precious bone—and they unravel. They start looking inward, questioning each other. That's when they fall."

"And Mittens?" Rex pressed. "What about him? Where does he fit into your little plan?"

Her gaze flickered, a shadow of something deeper passing across her features. "Mittens made his choice a long time ago," she said softly. "He chose power over loyalty, ambition over trust. He thought he could outsmart me, and for a time, he did. But he underestimated what I'm willing to do for this city."

Rex's eyes narrowed. "Sounds personal."

"It is," she admitted, her voice hardening. "Mittens betrayed me, just as he's betrayed everyone who's ever trusted him. But this isn't about revenge, Detective. It's about making things right."

Rex leaned back in his chair, his skepticism evident. "And you expect me to believe that? That you're doing all this for the greater good?"

Miss Whiskers tilted her head, her smile faint but knowing. "Believe what you want, Detective. But if you want to stop the Cartel, you'll keep following the trail I've laid out for you. Or walk away, if you're not up to the task."

Rex stood, his sharp eyes locked on hers. "I don't walk away from anything, Whiskers. But don't think for a second that I'm your pawn. You play me, and you'll regret it."

Her smile widened, though it still didn't reach her eyes. "I wouldn't dream of it."

Rex turned to leave, his mind racing. Her words lingered, heavy with implication, but so did the cracks in her facade. Miss Whiskers wasn't just a manipulator—she was a believer. And that made her dangerous.

As the elevator doors closed behind him, Rex's paw brushed against the notebook in his coat pocket. The glyphs, the Cartel, the bone—it was all connected, and Whiskers was at the center. But for all her talk of unity and justice, Rex couldn't shake the feeling that there was more to her story than she was letting on.

The city stretched out before him as the elevator descended, its lights a web of chaos and intrigue. Rex adjusted his hat, his jaw tightening with renewed determination. Whiskers might be holding the cards, but Rex wasn't about to let her deal him out of the game. Not yet.

The rain pattered against the wide windows of Miss Whiskers' penthouse, a muted soundtrack to the tense conversation unfolding inside. Rex Barkley stood near the doorway, arms crossed, his sharp eyes locked on Miss Whiskers. She sat gracefully on the edge of a velvet settee, her tail curling and uncurling in deliberate movements. The soft light from the chandelier above cast faint shadows across her face, highlighting the calm veneer she wore like armor.

"You think the Cartel's framing you?" Rex asked, his tone edged with skepticism. "That's convenient."

"It's the truth," Miss Whiskers replied smoothly, her voice even but not without a trace of exasperation. "You've seen their handiwork, haven't you? The staged robbery, the glyphs—none of it points to me."

Rex took a step closer, his boots clicking against the polished marble floor. "Sure, it doesn't. Not unless you're smart enough to make it look like someone else's handiwork."

She tilted her head, a faint smile tugging at her lips. "You give me far too much credit, Detective. If I had that kind of control, I wouldn't need to involve you."

"Maybe that's the point," Rex countered, his eyes narrowing. "You hire me to 'solve' the case, I chase the Cartel, and all the while, you stay out of the spotlight."

Miss Whiskers sighed, her tail flicking sharply. "Rex, if I wanted the Cartel out of the way, there are far more efficient methods than relying on you."

"Flattering," Rex muttered, leaning against the arm of a nearby chair. "So, let's hear it. Why would the Cartel bother framing you? What's the play?"

Miss Whiskers leaned forward, her claws resting lightly on her lap. "The Cartel thrives on fear and control. They don't just want power—they want obedience. And I've been... less than cooperative with their vision for Barkington."

"Less than cooperative?" Rex repeated, arching a brow. "What does that mean?"

"It means," she said, her voice dropping to a softer, more measured tone, "that I refused to bend. The Cartel wanted to use my connections, my influence, to strengthen their grip on this city. I said no."

Rex studied her carefully, his skepticism warring with a flicker of curiosity. "And now they're trying to take you down?"

Miss Whiskers nodded, her gaze steady. "If they can't control me, they'll destroy me. That's their way. They staged the robbery to make it look like I was desperate—like I was the one clawing for power."

"Or maybe you are," Rex said, not missing a beat.

Her eyes flashed, the first real crack in her composure. "You're impossible," she said sharply. "You think I'm lying? Fine. But tell me this, Detective—why would I risk everything just to play games with the Cartel? Do you think I enjoy living with a target on my back?"

"You don't strike me as the shrinking violet type," Rex replied. "You're too good at playing the angles."

Miss Whiskers rose gracefully from the settee, crossing the room to stand by the window. She stared out at the city lights, her reflection faint in the glass. When she spoke again, her voice was softer, almost vulnerable.

"You think this is a game for me?" she asked, her back still to Rex. "You think I enjoy the sleepless nights, the constant looking over my shoulder? I didn't ask for this, Rex. I've fought for everything I have, and now I'm fighting to keep it."

Rex straightened, his instincts tugging at him in conflicting directions. "You're good, Whiskers. Real good. But that doesn't mean you're telling the whole truth."

She turned to face him, her expression unreadable. "You don't trust me. I understand that. But you need to trust your own instincts. The Cartel doesn't just want me gone—they want you chasing shadows so you don't see the bigger picture."

"And what's that?" Rex asked, his voice low.

Miss Whiskers hesitated, her claws tapping lightly against her arm. "They're planning something. Something big. The bone was just the beginning—it's bait, Rex. They're trying to draw out every player in the city, force us to take sides."

Rex frowned, the weight of her words settling heavily. "And whose side are you on?"

"My own," she said simply, her gaze unwavering. "I don't need the Cartel, and I don't need their games. But if they think they can use me as a pawn, they're in for a rude awakening."

Rex took a slow step toward her, his voice firm. "If you're lying to me, Whiskers—if you're playing me like you're claiming they're playing you—I'll find out."

Her faint smile returned, though it carried a trace of sadness. "I wouldn't expect anything less from you, Detective."

The room fell silent for a moment, the tension thick enough to cut with a claw. Finally, Rex turned, heading for the door.

"You've given me a lot to think about," he said over his shoulder. "But I'm not taking your word for it."

"I wouldn't expect you to," she replied, her tone measured. "But be careful, Rex. The Cartel doesn't just deal in threats—they make good on them."

Rex didn't respond, his boots echoing against the marble floor as he left the penthouse. The elevator ride down was quiet, save for the hum of the machinery, but his thoughts were loud, each one a question chasing another. Was Miss Whiskers a victim, a manipulator, or both? The truth felt slippery, just out of reach. And if she was afraid, it meant the game was even more dangerous than he'd realized.

The elevator doors slid shut behind Rex Barkley with a soft hiss, enclosing him in a reflective steel box that hummed softly as it descended. His jaw tightened as he glanced at the faint reflection staring back at him. Miss Whiskers' words still lingered in the air around him, weaving between truth and manipulation. Her claim that the Cartel was framing her had the scent of desperation mixed with the sharp tang of misdirection. But buried in her smooth delivery was a sliver of something real. Fear? Maybe. Or maybe she was just good at faking it.

As the elevator reached the ground floor with a soft chime, Rex stepped out into the cool, damp night. The rain had finally stopped, leaving the city bathed in a slick sheen that reflected the glow of streetlights and neon signs. Rex lit a cigarette, the flick of his lighter echoing faintly as he took a drag, his thoughts churning.

Miss Whiskers' last words before he'd left had been cryptic yet deliberate. "The docks aren't where the Cartel makes their moves, Rex. Look west—where the lights stop, and the shadows take over."

"West," Rex muttered under his breath, exhaling a thin stream of smoke as he pulled out his notebook and jotted down the clue. "Where the lights stop. She really loves her riddles."

But west meant the abandoned industrial district, a stretch of decrepit warehouses and overgrown lots where the city's glow gave way to darkness. It made sense for the Cartel to hole up there—a place no one wanted to go and everyone knew better than to poke around in.

The faint scuff of footsteps to his left broke Rex's train of thought. He glanced up from his notebook, his sharp eyes scanning the damp sidewalk. A figure loitered near the edge of an alley, just barely visible in the dim light. Whoever it was wasn't doing a good job of being inconspicuous. Rex flicked his cigarette to the ground, grinding it out with the heel of his boot, and turned toward the figure.

"You waiting for an invitation, or are we going to have a conversation?" Rex called, his voice carrying just enough edge to make it clear he wasn't in the mood for games.

The figure stepped forward hesitantly, the weak glow of a streetlamp revealing a young calico cat, her fur matted and her eyes wide with unease. She was clutching a small parcel wrapped in brown paper, her claws digging into it as if it were a lifeline.

"You're Detective Barkley?" she asked, her voice trembling slightly.

"That depends," Rex said, taking a step closer. "Who's asking?"

"I... I work for the Cartel," she said quickly, her words tumbling out as if she couldn't stop them. "Or... I used to. They don't know I'm here."

Rex's eyes narrowed. "You've got about ten seconds to tell me why you're really here before I decide you're wasting my time."

The calico flinched but held her ground, thrusting the parcel toward him. "I'm here because you need to see this. They'll kill me if they find out, but... you have to know what they're planning."

Rex took the parcel cautiously, his fingers brushing against the damp paper. He studied her carefully, noting the way her tail flicked nervously, her ears twitching at every distant sound. She was terrified, but whether it was of him or the Cartel wasn't clear yet.

"What's in here?" he asked, his voice low.

"Documents," she said, her words barely above a whisper. "Blueprints. The Cartel's main hideout. It's not just a hideout—

it's where they keep everything. Their stash, their records... everything."

Rex frowned, his instincts buzzing. "Why give this to me? What's in it for you?"

"I just want out," she said, her eyes pleading. "I can't live like this anymore, always looking over my shoulder, always doing their dirty work. If you take them down, I'll finally be free."

Rex studied her for another moment, then nodded, tucking the parcel into his coat. "Get lost," he said, his tone curt. "And don't let me find out you're playing both sides."

She hesitated, her gaze flickering between Rex and the dark alley behind her. "Be careful, Detective. They're not like anyone you've gone up against before."

With that, she turned and disappeared into the shadows, her small form swallowed by the night. Rex stood there for a moment, the weight of the parcel pressing against his chest like a tangible reminder of the danger ahead.

The abandoned industrial district loomed large in his mind, the vague descriptions he'd heard over the years now taking on a sharper, more immediate form. If the Cartel had made it their base, it would be heavily fortified, crawling with thugs and enforcers. And yet, Rex couldn't shake the feeling that Miss Whiskers had known exactly what she was doing when she'd pointed him west.

"Where the lights stop," Rex muttered again, starting down the slick sidewalk. He pulled out his notebook, flipping to a fresh page as he walked. His doubts about Miss Whiskers grew with every step, her motivations as tangled as the city's alleys. Was she genuinely afraid of the Cartel, or was this just another layer of her game?

He jotted down her name alongside the other threads of the case: the staged robbery, the glyphs, the Cartel's shipments. Every piece pointed to a larger conspiracy, but the picture still wasn't clear.

Rex adjusted his hat, his pace quickening as he headed west. The parcel felt heavier with every step, its contents a potential key to unlocking the truth—or to leading him straight into a trap. Either way, he wasn't turning back. Not now. The city was watching, waiting, and Rex Barkley wasn't about to let it down.

Chapter 10
Symbols in the Rain

Rex Barkley didn't knock when he pushed open the door to **Commissioner Bowser's** office. The heavy oak slammed against the frame with a sharp crack that echoed off the sterile walls. The room smelled like old leather, cigar smoke, and power—a scent Bowser wore like armor. The mastiff sat behind his oversized desk, thick fingers wrapped around a half-smoked cigar, his eyes lifting slowly to meet Rex's.

"Barkley," Bowser growled, his tone as flat as the surface of the desk. "I thought I told you to let this go."

Rex didn't respond right away. He marched forward, trench coat still dripping from the rain, and dropped the **stolen ledger** onto the desk with a thud that rattled the commissioner's empty coffee mug. The mastiff's eyes flicked down to it for a half-second, but his face gave nothing away.

"Looks like you've been busy," Bowser said, leaning back in his chair. "Careful where you get your paws dirty, Barkley. Some stains don't come out."

"Save the advice," Rex growled, his voice low and sharp. "I found this at Bentley Poodle's little sardine auction. It's a ledger, Bowser—shipments, payoffs, and a whole lot of dirty laundry. You know what name I didn't see in here?"

Bowser exhaled a long stream of smoke, feigning calm. "I'm sure you're about to tell me."

"Yours." Rex jabbed a finger at the ledger, his glare cold and unrelenting. "Funny, isn't it? The Kennel Club and the Alley Cartel are clawing at each other's throats, and yet you—the one guy who should be keeping this city clean—come out smelling like roses. Smells wrong to me, Bowser."

Bowser's expression darkened, and for a moment, Rex thought the mastiff might snap. Instead, he stubbed the cigar out in a glass ashtray, the ember hissing faintly. "You're making accusations you can't back up, Barkley."

"Accusations?" Rex barked out a humorless laugh. "Cut the act. I don't have time for it. The bone—the *Diamond Key*—opens a vault full of evidence that could bury the Kennel Club and the Cartel both. And you've been doing everything you can to keep me off their trail. So what is it, Bowser? What have they got on you?"

For the first time, Bowser's mask cracked. His jaw tightened, his paws gripping the arms of his chair like he was holding himself back from snapping the desk in two. He stared at Rex for a long moment, the tension thick enough to choke on.

Finally, he spoke, his voice quieter but no less menacing. "You think you know what's going on in this city, Barkley? You don't. You've been chasing ghosts and half-truths, and you don't have the slightest idea what it costs to keep this place from burning down."

"Then tell me," Rex shot back, leaning over the desk. "What's the price, Bowser? How much does it take to sell your soul?"

Bowser's gaze was like stone, but his voice shook faintly at the edges. "They've got my family, Rex. You understand that? The Kennel Club—they found a way in. Pictures, documents… things I didn't even know they knew about. If I don't play nice, my family pays the price."

Rex froze, the words hitting him harder than any punch. "Your family?"

Bowser looked away, his shoulders slumping for the first time. "You think I like this? That I *chose* this? I'm in their pocket because they backed me into it. I keep the peace—just enough to keep my head above water. But this isn't a war you win, Barkley. It's one you survive."

Rex straightened slowly, his fists clenching at his sides. The anger bubbling in his chest wasn't just for Bowser—it was for the whole rotten system. The Kennel Club pulling strings. The Alley Cartel fighting for control. And good dogs like Bowser twisted until they broke.

"So that's it?" Rex asked, his voice low and bitter. "You just roll over and let them run the show? Let the rest of us drown while you stay afloat?"

Bowser's head snapped up, his eyes blazing. "You don't get it. They're too big, Rex. The Cartel. The Kennel Club. The Council pulling strings behind them both. You think one hound with a trench coat and a bad attitude can change any of that? You'll end up dead before you even scratch the surface."

"Maybe," Rex said, his voice steady as steel. "But someone's gotta try. Someone's gotta stand up and tell these bastards their time's up."

Bowser laughed bitterly, a sound that held no humor. "You're a stubborn fool, Barkley. You always were."

Rex grabbed the ledger off the desk and shoved it back into his coat. "And you're a coward, Bowser. You always will be."

The two locked eyes, the silence heavy and sharp between them. For a second, Rex thought Bowser might try to stop him, but the mastiff just slumped back in his chair, his face carved with defeat.

As Rex turned to leave, Bowser's voice rumbled one last warning. "Walk away, Barkley. You think you're chasing justice, but all you'll find is a bullet with your name on it."

Rex paused at the door, his paw on the handle. He glanced back over his shoulder, his eyes cold. "Maybe. But I'll sleep better knowing I wasn't the one who let this city rot."

The door closed behind him with a heavy thud, leaving Bowser alone in the silence of his office. The rain outside hadn't let up, and as Rex stepped back into the night, he felt the weight of everything he'd learned pressing down on him like a lead coat.

Bowser was right about one thing—the Kennel Club and the Cartel were too big. But Rex didn't care. The ledger under his coat was proof, and now that he knew the truth, there was no turning back.

"Someone's gotta bring this house down," Rex muttered to himself, his breath fogging in the cold. "Might as well be me."

The rain was still falling when Rex Barkley made his way through the grimy back alleys that led to **The Scratch Post**, the Alley Cartel's headquarters. It was a building that looked like it had been stitched together out of forgotten bricks and broken promises, perched like a mangy cat at the edge of Barkington's underbelly. Rex had never been welcome here, and tonight wouldn't be any different. But he was out of options.

Mittens Malone didn't *trust*, and Rex didn't *ask*. That's just how things worked between them.

Rex stepped up to the steel door, its paint peeling and rust creeping up the sides. He knocked hard, the sound echoing like a gunshot in the quiet. After a moment, a slit slid open at eye level, and a pair of bloodshot feline eyes narrowed at him.

"Who's asking?" the voice hissed.

"Tell Mittens it's Barkley," Rex growled. "I've got something he wants."

The eyes lingered, suspicious, but the slit slammed shut. Rex waited, his ears tuned to the faint sounds of shifting furniture and footsteps behind the door. Finally, with a grating *clang,* the lock turned, and the door creaked open.

"Through here, hound," the thug muttered, jerking his head toward the dark corridor beyond.

Rex stepped inside, his nose immediately assaulted by the sharp smell of old catnip and unwashed fur. He pushed forward, past stacks of crates and lounging Cartel enforcers who stared at him like he'd just wandered into a lion's den.

At the far end of the room sat **Mittens Malone**, sprawled lazily in a cracked leather armchair. The tabby's yellow eyes gleamed in the dim light, his sharp claws tapping against the armrest. A smug grin crept onto his face as he watched Rex approach.

"Well, well, look what the rain dragged in," Mittens purred, sitting up just slightly. "Rex Barkley. I thought you had better sense than to come scratching at my door."

"I'm short on options," Rex replied, stopping just short of the desk that separated them. "And you're short on friends, Mittens. So let's not pretend we're not both desperate here."

Mittens' grin faltered, replaced by a calculating look. "Desperation suits you, hound. But what makes you think I need *you?*"

Rex reached into his coat and pulled out the ledger, slapping it down onto the table between them. Mittens' ears flicked forward, his claws stilling as he eyed the worn cover.

"Bentley Poodle's ledger," Rex said flatly. "I found it at the sardine auction. It's got everything—shipments, payoffs, and the bone's connection to the vault. The Kennel Club's making their move, Mittens. And you're running out of time to stop them."

Mittens narrowed his eyes, his tone low and measured. "What do you want, Barkley?"

"I want what you want," Rex said, locking eyes with him. "To stop Miss Whiskers before she uses the bone to take control of that vault. You and I both know what happens if she wins."

Mittens' tail flicked once, sharp and deliberate. "You expect me to believe you're doing this out of the goodness of your heart?"

Rex let out a bitter laugh. "Goodness died in this city a long time ago. I'm doing it because if she gets that bone, the Kennel Club ends up holding all the cards. You think they'll leave room for the Alley Cartel in their new kingdom?"

Mittens' claws flexed against the leather armrest. He said nothing, but his eyes burned with a frustration Rex had counted on.

"She played us both, Mittens," Rex continued. "You told me yourself—she's smart, too smart. The whole helpless act? She was setting me up, and I'd bet every kibble I've got she's been setting you up, too. You want revenge? Fine. I want the truth. But we're not going to get either unless we work together."

Mittens leaned back in his chair, the tension crackling between them like a live wire. Finally, he spoke, his voice a low rumble. "You've got guts, hound. I'll give you that. But you and me? We don't *work together.*"

"We do tonight," Rex shot back. "Unless you've got another plan I don't know about. You want to go after Whiskers blind, be my guest. But if you're smart—and I know you are—you'll take the help."

Mittens sat silent for a moment, his yellow eyes locked onto Rex's, the wheels turning behind them. Around them, the room felt heavier, the Cartel enforcers watching with open curiosity as their boss weighed his options. Finally, Mittens let out a slow, humorless chuckle.

"You've got a hell of a mouth, Barkley," Mittens said, standing and smoothing down his fur. "Fine. We'll play this your way— for now. But understand this: if you cross me, if this turns out to be another one of your stunts, I'll make sure you regret ever stepping paw into my territory."

Rex didn't flinch. "Noted. But if you try to double-cross me, Mittens, you won't like how it ends either."

Mittens grinned, showing just a hint of fang. "Deal. Now tell me what you've got."

Rex leaned forward, planting his paws on the desk. "The bone's being moved again. The docks, midnight. Miss Whiskers will be there, and we both know she won't come unprepared. Bring your muscle—just make sure they don't get in my way."

Mittens' tail swished slowly behind him, his grin lingering. "Oh, don't worry, Barkley. I'll bring enough claws to tear the whole place apart."

Rex straightened, tucking the ledger back into his coat. He turned toward the door, Mittens' voice following him out.

"You'd better pray this works, hound. Because if it doesn't, you're the first one I'm coming for."

Rex didn't bother looking back. "Get in line."

As the steel door clanged shut behind him, Rex exhaled slowly. He'd struck a deal with a devil tonight, but he didn't care. The clock was ticking, and if they didn't stop Miss Whiskers soon, there wouldn't be a city left to save.

He pulled his collar up against the rain and disappeared into the dark, the uneasy alliance settling like a stone in his gut.

The rain came down harder as Rex Barkley stepped out of **The Scratch Post,** his breath a steady plume of mist in the cold night air. Beside him, **Mittens Malone** prowled like a shadow, his claws clicking faintly against the pavement. The uneasy silence stretched between them, both hounds and cats alike knowing that words wouldn't smooth the jagged edges of their alliance.

"She's making her move, Barkley," Mittens said suddenly, breaking the quiet. His voice was a low growl, his tone sharp as a blade. "We're running out of time."

Rex's ears flicked toward him, his trench coat whipping around his legs as the wind picked up. "You've got something?"

Mittens shot him a sidelong glance, his yellow eyes glinting in the dim glow of a streetlamp. "One of my scouts—Rook— picked up word at the docks. Miss Whiskers is making her play *tonight*. Midnight sharp."

Rex's jaw tightened. "She's going for the vault."

"Yeah," Mittens confirmed, his tail twitching. "She's not hiding anymore. She's pulling out all the stops. Heavy muscle, tight operation—she's got her sights set on that bone and everything it unlocks."

Rex turned the information over in his head, the ledger still weighing heavy in his coat pocket. It wasn't just about the bone anymore. The vault was more than a treasure chest—it was a loaded weapon. Whoever controlled it could tip the scales, and the city would burn for it.

Mittens slowed his pace, stopping just beneath an awning that barely shielded them from the rain. "Here's what I don't get, Barkley," he said, studying Rex with a suspicious gleam in his eye. "Why are *you* so worked up about this? What's a dirty vault full of secrets to a mutt like you?"

Rex turned to face him, rain streaking down his hat brim and into the deep lines of his face. "Because this city's already hanging by a thread. You cut that thread, Mittens, and it's chaos. The kind of chaos that doesn't get put back together."

Mittens scoffed, baring a hint of fang. "Chaos ain't so bad. You get rid of the weak links. Survival of the fittest, right?"

"Not when it tears down the whole damn house," Rex shot back, his voice gravelly and low. "I'm no saint, Malone. But I don't like watching innocent dogs and cats bleed just so someone else can sit on the throne."

Mittens stared at him for a long moment, his expression unreadable, before finally snorting. "You've got a funny way of looking at the world, Barkley. But fine. You wanna play hero? Play hero. Just don't get in my way when the claws come out."

"We're on the same side—*for now*," Rex reminded him. "You want to stop Whiskers, so do I. But when this is over, I'll make sure no one gets their paws on that vault."

"Big talk for a mutt without an army," Mittens said, but there was no bite in his voice. "What's your plan, then?"

Rex paused, the gears turning in his head. The docks were a labyrinth—old warehouses, forgotten shipping crates, and too many corners for someone like Miss Whiskers to hide in. She wouldn't go in alone; she'd have backup, and plenty of it.

"We split up," Rex said finally, his voice firm. "You bring your muscle—whatever you've got left—and come at her head-on. She'll expect that. While you're keeping her busy, I'll find the bone and stop her from opening the vault."

Mittens arched an eyebrow, his tail swishing sharply. "And what makes you think I'll leave the bone in *your* paws when this is over?"

Rex smirked faintly. "Because you're smart enough to know I'm your best shot at getting it before Whiskers does. That's the deal, isn't it?"

Mittens' eyes narrowed, but he didn't argue. "Fine," he said after a beat. "You'd better be quick, Barkley. Whiskers plays dirty, and if you're still sniffing around when things go south, I won't come looking for you."

"Don't worry about me," Rex muttered, adjusting his hat as he turned toward the street. "Just keep your end of the bargain."

Mittens watched him for a moment, the rain running in rivulets down his whiskers. "You're a real stubborn piece of work, you know that?"

"Yeah," Rex said without looking back. "So I've been told."

The two of them stood for a second longer, rain pattering in the silence like the ticking of a clock. It wasn't trust between them—nothing so fragile—but it was something close enough for tonight.

"Midnight," Mittens said, his voice a low rumble. "Don't be late, Barkley."

Rex tipped his hat and disappeared into the rain, his silhouette swallowed by the shadows of the city.

The docks were waiting for him, and Miss Whiskers was already on the move. The pieces were falling into place, but the game wasn't over yet. Rex could feel it in his bones—whatever happened tonight, there'd be no coming back from it.

And for a hound like him, that was just fine.

Chapter 11
Underworld Secrets

Rex Barkley sat at his desk, a half-empty glass of cheap whiskey in front of him and the hum of the city crawling through the cracks in his office window. The rain had let up, but the air still carried the weight of something heavy and unresolved, like the calm before a storm. His mind was a whirl of leads, double-crosses, and the uneasy alliance he'd struck with Mittens Malone. He didn't like it, but the clock was ticking, and in Barkington, time was something you never had enough of.

The envelope sat dead center on his desk, cream-colored and pristine, a sharp contrast to the chaos surrounding it. Rex had found it slipped under his door not five minutes ago, and it reeked of trouble. The handwriting on the front—smooth, flowing cursive—was unmistakable. **Miss Whiskers.**

"Never could keep your claws out of the game, could you?" Rex muttered, picking it up and sliding a claw under the flap.

Inside was a single sheet of paper, the message short and cryptic, exactly the kind of thing he expected from her:

"The answers you're sniffing for are waiting. Abandoned Warehouse, Pier 19. Midnight. Come alone. —W."

Rex stared at the note for a long moment, his nose twitching as if trying to sniff out the layers of deceit buried in the ink. It was classic Miss Whiskers—leading him just far enough to keep him guessing, just close enough to keep him on her trail.

His gut screamed at him to ignore it. Everything about it stank like a week-old fish left in the sun. She was up to something. She *always* was. But Rex couldn't shake the feeling that if he didn't go, he'd be leaving a piece of the puzzle on the table.

"Damn it," he muttered, pushing himself up from the chair. His coat was still damp when he shrugged it on, the trench heavier than it felt that morning.

The abandoned warehouse at **Pier 19** loomed like a forgotten monolith, its hulking frame silhouetted against the glow of the distant dock lights. The air here was colder, sharper, and carried the tang of salt and rust. It was the kind of place where promises broke, where bodies turned up face-down in the river and no one asked questions.

Rex paused just outside the warehouse, his paw hovering over the rusted door handle. He could feel the stillness inside—it was too quiet, the kind of silence that had teeth.

"You know this is a trap," his instincts growled. "But you're going in anyway."

He pushed the door open, the hinges groaning loud enough to wake the dead. The warehouse swallowed him whole as he stepped inside, his boots crunching against scattered debris. A single light flickered overhead, casting weak shadows on the cracked concrete floor.

"Whiskers?" Rex called out, his voice echoing through the cavernous space. "If this is your idea of a meeting spot, I've got notes."

Silence.

He scanned the room, his eyes narrowing as he moved deeper into the warehouse. Stacks of old crates were piled high, their labels faded and peeling. The air felt heavy, thick with dust and secrets, and Rex's nose picked up faint traces of catnip and oil—like someone had been here recently, but not long enough to leave a trail.

"You came," a voice purred from somewhere above him.

Rex froze, ears twitching. He tilted his head upward to see **Miss Whiskers** perched elegantly on a steel catwalk, her figure silhouetted against the light streaming through a cracked window. She was calm, poised, her diamond collar catching the faint light like a constellation.

"Could've sent flowers instead of cryptic notes," Rex called back, his voice edged with gravel. "Would've saved me a trip."

Miss Whiskers stepped forward, her movements smooth as silk. "You always were predictable, Rex. I knew you couldn't resist."

"Yeah?" Rex's paw hovered near the inside of his coat. "I almost stayed home. My gut told me this was a setup."

She tilted her head, her expression unreadable. "Is that why you came alone?"

"Didn't figure you'd want a crowd," Rex shot back. "So what's this about, Whiskers? You didn't drag me down here just for small talk."

Miss Whiskers leaned casually against the railing, her blue eyes gleaming faintly. "What if I told you I wanted to help you, Rex? That we both want the same thing."

Rex snorted. "You'll forgive me if I don't buy the damsel routine. You've already got Mittens clawing at your tail and the Kennel Club wrapped around your paw. Why play nice with me?"

She smiled faintly, the kind of smile that could cut glass. "Because you're the only one who doesn't know how to quit. The others—Malone, Bowser—they're too compromised. You're reckless enough to get close to the truth."

Rex's eyes narrowed. "What truth?"

Miss Whiskers stepped closer, her voice dropping just enough to make him strain to hear. "The bone, Rex. It's not just about the vault. It's about *control*. Whoever has that key holds the city's leash, and they'll choke the life out of anyone who gets in their way. I'm trying to make sure that doesn't happen."

"And you're the good guy in this story?" Rex shot back, skepticism thick in his voice.

"Call it survival," she purred. "But here's the thing, Rex—I'm not the one you should be worried about. There's someone else pulling strings in the shadows, and if you don't move fast, you'll never see them coming."

Rex's fur bristled. "And who's that?"

Miss Whiskers straightened, her voice smooth but sharp as steel. "I can't tell you yet. Not until I know I can trust you."

"You're out of luck, Whiskers," Rex growled. "Trust is in short supply tonight."

The lights flickered suddenly, and Miss Whiskers' expression shifted—just for a second, just enough to show something Rex didn't expect. Fear.

"Rex—" she started.

The sound of footsteps erupted from the far end of the warehouse. Heavy, fast, and coming straight for him. Rex's instincts fired like a starting gun.

"Trap," he muttered.

Miss Whiskers' voice cut through the noise, sharp and urgent. "Get out of here, Rex! *Now!*"

He didn't argue. The shadows were moving, figures spilling out from the dark like ink on a blank page. Rex spun, his boots pounding against the floor as he bolted for the door, his breath quick and controlled. Behind him, the first shot rang out, splintering the crate he'd just passed.

"Damn it," Rex growled, weaving through the maze of debris as the warehouse exploded into chaos.

Miss Whiskers' voice echoed faintly in the back of his mind, her words cutting through the noise like a blade.

"There's someone else pulling the strings."

Rex didn't have time to process it. Whoever it was, they were closer than he thought—and they weren't playing fair.

Rex Barkley moved through the maze of debris, his boots sliding across the slick concrete floor as shadows closed in behind him. The air in the abandoned warehouse was thick with tension, every step echoing like a warning shot in the cavernous space. He knew it had been a trap the moment the lights flickered—just a second too long for it to be coincidence. Miss Whiskers' words still rattled in his head, but there was no time to sift through them now.

The scuffle of feet—no, **paws**—rushed toward him from both flanks, like a noose tightening around his neck. They were quick, quiet, but Rex's ears caught every shift, every intake of breath.

"Out of the frying pan," Rex muttered, his hand brushing the inside of his coat where his revolver waited.

Before he could draw, two figures leapt out from the dark, feline silhouettes cutting through the shadows. The first—a wiry calico with a snarl sharp enough to split stone—lunged straight for him. Rex twisted at the last second, the thug's claws raking the air where his chest had been. Rex brought his elbow up and slammed it into the calico's ribs with a satisfying crack, sending him sprawling into a pile of crates.

"Too slow," Rex growled, his words lost in the chaos.

Another figure was on him before he could recover—this one a hulking black tomcat, muscle where finesse should've been. The thug swung hard, a blunt object clutched in his paw—a crowbar, dull and heavy. Rex ducked, the whoosh of the swing slicing the air above him. He came up fast, his fist connecting with the tomcat's jaw, but it was like punching a brick wall.

The tomcat grinned, shaking it off like nothing had happened. "That all you got, mutt?"

Rex grunted as he was shoved backward, slamming into a rusted support beam with enough force to knock the wind out of him. His vision blurred for a second, the shadows swimming, but instinct carried him through. He staggered sideways, dodging another swing of the crowbar, and ripped the revolver from his coat.

"Back off!" Rex barked, his voice like thunder, the muzzle of the gun gleaming under the dim overhead light.

For a moment, the black tomcat hesitated, ears flicking toward the weapon. But before Rex could line up a shot, a heavy weight collided with him from behind—another hench-cat, claws digging into his shoulder as they crashed to the ground in a heap. The gun skittered across the floor, clattering into the dark, just out of reach.

"Three against one?" Rex growled through gritted teeth. "Real brave."

The calico scrambled to his feet, wiping blood from the corner of his mouth. "You should've stayed out of it, Barkley. You think Miss Whiskers wants you sniffing around her business?"

Rex twisted hard, throwing the cat on his back off just enough to roll free. He staggered up, breathing hard, pain shooting through his ribs where he'd taken the hit. "Funny," Rex rasped, his voice low, "I was starting to think Whiskers wanted me alive."

The black tomcat stepped forward again, the crowbar swinging loosely in his paw. "She said you could leave. You didn't listen."

"Listening's never been my strong suit," Rex shot back.

The tomcat lunged, the crowbar slicing through the air again. Rex dodged sideways, barely keeping his balance as his boots slid across the rain-slicked floor. He grabbed a length of broken pipe leaning against the crates and swung it hard, the sharp clang of metal against metal reverberating through the warehouse. Sparks shot off the crowbar as it struck the pipe, but Rex didn't stop. He twisted low and swung for the tomcat's knee.

The thug howled as the blow connected, dropping him to the floor with a heavy thud. Rex didn't wait. He turned and ran for the far end of the warehouse, his breath coming in sharp bursts, the sound of pursuit echoing close behind.

"Don't let him get out!" the calico shouted, his voice sharp and ragged.

Rex sprinted through the shadows, weaving between crates as the faint glow of an exit sign came into view. Every muscle screamed as he pushed forward, every breath burning in his chest. Another shot rang out, shattering glass somewhere above his head. He didn't look back.

He reached the door just as a clawed paw snagged his coat. With a snarl, Rex yanked free, stumbling into the rain-drenched alley outside. He slammed the door shut behind him, the thud echoing like punctuation. He didn't stop moving until he'd put two full blocks between him and the warehouse, the shadows of the docks stretching long and quiet under the streetlights.

Rex collapsed against a brick wall, sucking in ragged breaths as he clutched his side. Blood dampened his shirt—nothing fatal, but enough to remind him how close he'd been to not walking out of that place.

He tilted his head back, rain streaming down his face, and let out a bitter chuckle. "You almost got me, Whiskers," he muttered, his voice hoarse. "Almost."

But as the adrenaline ebbed, Rex's mind started working again, replaying the words those thugs had barked. *She said you could leave. You didn't listen.*

Miss Whiskers hadn't wanted him dead—at least, not yet. Which meant there was still something she needed him for. And if that was the case, Rex had a feeling he wasn't out of the trap just yet.

He pulled himself upright, wincing as he straightened. The storm wasn't over—it was just getting started. And if Miss Whiskers thought she could play him, she was about to find out just how wrong she was.

Rex Barkley limped through the rain-soaked streets of Barkington, his trench coat clinging to his frame like dead weight. His ribs throbbed with every step, and his shoulder burned where claws had found purchase. Blood had dried into dark streaks under his collar, and the sharp ache in his side told him he'd be nursing bruises for weeks. It wasn't the pain that weighed him down, though. It was the truth—the ugly, undeniable truth—that Miss Whiskers had been playing him from the start.

By the time Rex reached his office building, the city had gone quiet, the kind of eerie stillness that only came at the deepest hours of the night. He pushed open the door to the narrow stairwell, his boots echoing against the creaking steps as he dragged himself up to the third floor. He didn't stop at the door, didn't hesitate as he shoved it open and let it slam shut behind him.

The office was cold, dark, and lifeless—just the way he'd left it. The faint glow of the city beyond his window lit up the room in streaks of pale gray, cutting through the dust and cigarette smoke lingering in the air. Rex staggered toward his desk and sank heavily into the chair, leaning back with a sharp hiss as his ribs protested the movement.

For a long minute, he sat in silence, his eyes fixed on the ceiling as rain drummed softly against the glass. Then, slowly, he leaned forward and rested his elbows on his desk, burying his face in his paws.

"You've been played, Barkley," he muttered to himself, the words coming bitter and low. "Hook, line, and sinker."

The words burned, but they were true. Miss Whiskers—damn her—had seen him coming from a mile away. She'd lured him in with charm and desperation, fed him half-truths and let him follow the trail like a good little bloodhound. All the while, she'd been pulling strings from the shadows, keeping him just close enough to feel like he had a shot at the truth, but far enough away to stay in control.

Rex slammed his fist onto the desk, the sound a sharp crack in the empty room. Papers scattered, an old coffee mug rattled, and for a moment, he just sat there, glaring at nothing in particular. His reflection stared back at him from the rain-streaked window—a tired bloodhound with a face full of bruises and eyes that didn't look like they trusted anyone anymore.

"Played me for a fool," Rex muttered, shaking his head. "The whole time."

His mind replayed every step of the case: Miss Whiskers slinking into his office that first night, her voice smooth as silk and dripping with just the right amount of vulnerability. The stolen bone, the breadcrumbs she'd left him—Mittens Malone, the Kennel Club, and the ledger. She'd given him just enough to keep chasing, enough to make him believe she was another victim in a city built on power plays and backstabbing.

Rex's fists curled tight against the desk. "You almost had me, Whiskers. Almost."

The worst part—the part he hated himself for—was the sliver of doubt that lingered in his gut. There had been moments, fleeting but real, where he'd seen something in her eyes that wasn't manipulation. Maybe it was fear. Maybe it was guilt. Or maybe he'd just wanted to see it, wanted to believe that even someone like her had a line she wouldn't cross.

"Sentimental mutt," he growled under his breath, reaching for the half-empty bottle of whiskey tucked in the bottom drawer. He poured a measure into his glass and watched it swirl before taking a long drink. It burned all the way down, but it didn't drown the feeling clawing at the back of his mind.

She'd played him, and it stung. Not just because it made him look like a fool, but because he'd let her get close enough to do it. For a hound like Rex Barkley, trust wasn't something he handed out freely, and when someone broke it, they didn't get a second chance.

He sat there for a moment longer, the whiskey settling in his gut as the rain drummed harder against the glass. Then, slowly, he pushed himself to his feet, grimacing at the ache in his ribs. He grabbed his hat off the rack and pulled it low over his eyes, his expression hard as stone.

"Alright, Whiskers," he muttered, his voice low and gravelly. "You've had your fun. Now it's my turn."

He crossed the room in a few steady strides, pulling open the filing cabinet against the far wall. He thumbed through the folders until he found the one he was looking for—a thin file marked **'W.'** It wasn't much, just scraps of intel and old reports he'd collected over the years, but it was enough to remind him of who he was dealing with.

Rex flipped the file open, his eyes scanning the notes, the photos, the names connected to her past. She was smart, he'd give her that. But even the smartest cats left trails when they ran.

"I don't care how long it takes," Rex growled, tucking the file under his arm as he moved toward the door. "I'm finishing this case. You hear me, Whiskers? I'm finishing it."

He stepped back out into the rain, the cold wind biting through his coat, but he didn't feel it. The game had changed tonight. The stakes were higher, the trust was shattered, and Rex Barkley had nothing left to lose.

As he melted into the dark streets of Barkington, his silhouette lost against the mist and shadows, Rex let the thought settle in his mind like a promise. Miss Whiskers might have been playing him from the start, but the end?

The end would belong to him.

Chapter 12
The Bone's True Weight

The abandoned industrial district stretched out before Rex Barkley like a graveyard for forgotten ambition. Broken windows, rusted fences, and graffiti-covered walls marked the territory, but it was the eerie quiet that set his nerves on edge. Somewhere in this maze of decay lay the Cartel's hideout—a fortress of shadows and secrets.

Rex adjusted his hat, his sharp eyes scanning the perimeter of the warehouse he'd identified from the blueprints. The parcel he'd received had proven invaluable, outlining the building's layout and the paths least likely to be patrolled. Still, Rex knew better than to trust a map alone. The Cartel wasn't in the business of making things easy.

He crouched low as he approached the back entrance, his boots silent against the cracked pavement. The scent of fish oil was stronger now, mingling with the metallic tang of rust and the faint aroma of damp wood. Rex's nose twitched as he reached the door, his paw brushing against the handle.

Locked. Of course.

Rex pulled a set of slim lockpicks from his coat pocket, his movements quick and practiced. Within moments, the lock gave way with a soft click. He eased the door open, slipping inside and closing it silently behind him.

The warehouse interior was dimly lit, the faint glow of hanging bulbs casting long shadows across stacks of crates and metal shelving. Voices drifted from somewhere deeper inside, their words muffled but laced with tension.

"Keep it moving. The boss doesn't want any delays."

"Yeah, yeah. You think I want to be here any longer than I have to?"

Rex crept along the edges of the room, his ears straining to catch every word. The blueprints had indicated an office on the second floor, and if the Cartel was keeping records of their operation, that's where they'd be. He moved quickly but cautiously, his steps measured to avoid the creaking floorboards.

As he climbed the metal staircase, the voices grew fainter, replaced by the distant hum of machinery and the occasional clang of metal on metal. The office door was ajar, and Rex paused just outside, his sharp eyes scanning the interior. The room was sparsely furnished—just a desk, a filing cabinet, and a few scattered papers—but it was the map pinned to the wall that caught his attention.

The map of Barkington was marked with a series of red X's, each one corresponding to a known Cartel hotspot. But at the center, circled in bold red ink, was a name that made Rex's ears twitch: **Miss Whiskers.**

He stepped inside, his eyes narrowing as he took in the scene. The desk was cluttered with documents, and Rex began sifting through them, his sharp nose catching the faint scent of fish oil and ink. A ledger caught his attention, its pages filled with lists of shipments, payments, and coded messages. But one entry stood out—a note scrawled in the margin:

"Bone acquired. Leverage secured. Await orders from HQ."

"Leverage," Rex muttered, his voice barely audible. "They're using the bone to blackmail her."

The creak of a floorboard behind him made Rex freeze. He turned just in time to see a shadow looming in the doorway— a burly Maine Coon with a scar running across his muzzle. The cat's eyes narrowed as he took in the scene.

"Well, well," the Maine Coon drawled, his voice thick with disdain. "Look what the rain dragged in."

"Nice place you've got here," Rex said, his tone casual despite the tension. "Though I've got to say, your filing system needs work."

The Maine Coon stepped into the room, his claws flexing. "You've got a lot of nerve, hound. Breaking in, poking around where you don't belong. You know what we do to trespassers?"

"I can guess," Rex replied, his paw hovering near the edge of his coat. "But I'm not here for a fight. Just a few answers."

"Answers?" The Maine Coon laughed, a low, guttural sound. "You've got it all wrong, pal. The only thing you're getting is a one-way ticket out of here—feet first."

Before the Maine Coon could move, Rex lunged forward, slamming the desk into the cat's legs and sending him sprawling. Papers scattered as Rex grabbed the ledger and bolted for the door, the Maine Coon's snarls echoing behind him.

"Get him!" the Maine Coon roared, his voice carrying through the warehouse.

Rex sprinted down the stairs, his boots pounding against the metal. The sound of footsteps and angry shouts filled the air as the Cartel's goons gave chase. He darted between crates and machinery, his sharp instincts guiding him through the maze-like interior.

A stack of crates to his left toppled as one of the thugs lunged for him, but Rex was faster, slipping through a narrow gap and emerging near the back entrance. He burst through the door into the night, the cool air a sharp contrast to the stifling tension inside.

Rex didn't stop running until he was several blocks away, his breath coming in sharp bursts as he leaned against a brick wall. The ledger was clutched tightly in his paw, its pages the key to unraveling the Cartel's plan.

They were using the bone as leverage, a tool to control Miss Whiskers and cement their power. But the bigger question remained: why had Miss Whiskers let the bone fall into their hands in the first place? Was it a calculated risk, or had the Cartel outmaneuvered her?

Rex adjusted his hat, his jaw tightening as he straightened. The pieces were falling into place, but the picture they formed was darker than he'd anticipated. The Cartel wasn't just running a criminal empire—they were playing for keeps. And Rex Barkley wasn't about to fold. Not now.

The damp air inside the abandoned warehouse clung to Rex Barkley's coat as he crouched in a dim corner, the stolen ledger tucked under one arm and the prized bone clutched in his paw. The room was quiet now, save for the faint hum of a generator somewhere deep in the building. He had barely escaped the Cartel's claws, and the evidence he'd snatched was heavy with implications. But it wasn't just the ledger that had his attention. It was the bone.

The diamond-encrusted heirloom felt oddly weighted in his paw, its smooth surface cool against his pads. Rex's sharp eyes scanned the intricate carvings along its length, his instincts buzzing. This wasn't just a flashy symbol—it was something more.

"Alright," Rex muttered to himself, setting the bone down on a crate under the faint glow of a dangling light bulb. "Let's see what secrets you're hiding."

As his claws traced the carvings, he noticed subtle irregularities—grooves that didn't match the decorative patterns. He pressed against one, and to his surprise, it shifted under the pressure. A faint click echoed in the still air, and a hidden compartment slid open along the bone's underside.

"Well, I'll be," Rex murmured, his breath catching as he peered inside.

Tucked within the hollowed-out space was a folded sheet of paper, its edges worn but its content unmistakably deliberate. Rex carefully unfolded it, the faint scent of ink wafting up as he spread it out on the crate. His eyes darted across the intricate map drawn on the paper, its lines and markings revealing a web of connections across Barkington.

At the center of the map was a glyph—the same symbol he'd seen at the penthouse and the docks. Surrounding it were notes scrawled in sharp handwriting, detailing locations, shipments, and dates. But it was the word at the bottom, underlined with a heavy hand, that made Rex's ears twitch.

Dominion.

"Dominion?" Rex said aloud, his voice laced with curiosity and unease. "What the hell are they planning?"

The sound of soft footsteps behind him made him spin, his paw instinctively reaching for his flashlight. Standing in the doorway was a wiry Siamese cat, her fur matted and her eyes wide with fear. She raised her paws, signaling she wasn't a threat.

"Easy, Detective," she said, her voice low. "I'm not here to fight."

"Then start talking," Rex growled, keeping his distance. "Who sent you?"

"Nobody," the cat replied, her tone urgent. "I heard the commotion. I know what you're holding, and you need to get out of here before they come back."

Rex narrowed his eyes, his grip tightening on the map. "You seem awfully well-informed for someone just passing by."

The Siamese hesitated, her tail flicking nervously. "I used to run with the Cartel," she admitted. "I know how they operate, and I know what that bone means. If they find out you've got it..."

"They already know," Rex cut in, his voice sharp. "What I need to know is what *Dominion* means. Start explaining, or I'll assume you're stalling for time."

The cat glanced around, her ears twitching at every distant sound. "Dominion isn't just a plan," she said finally. "It's the Cartel's endgame. They're not content with controlling the city anymore—they want everything. Every district, every rival gang, every ounce of power.”

“And the bone?” Rex pressed. “How does it fit in?”

“It’s a symbol,” she said, stepping closer. “But it’s also a key. That map you’re holding? It doesn’t just show locations—it shows leverage. Secrets, blackmail material, everything the Cartel’s been using to stay on top. With that, they can consolidate power and crush anyone who stands in their way.”

Rex’s jaw tightened as he processed her words. “And Miss Whiskers? Where does she fit into this?”

The Siamese hesitated, her expression unreadable. “She’s not innocent, Detective. But she’s not the one pulling the strings here. The Cartel framed her to keep you off their trail, but she’s as much a pawn as the rest of us.”

Rex didn’t like the way the pieces were falling into place. The bone wasn’t just leverage—it was a weapon, and the Cartel was preparing to use it to reshape the city in their image. Miss Whiskers’ manipulations suddenly seemed smaller, her schemes eclipsed by the sheer scale of the Cartel’s ambition.

“Why help me?” Rex asked, his voice hard. “You could’ve walked away.”

The Siamese met his gaze, her eyes steady despite the fear in her posture. “Because I’m tired of running,” she said simply. “And if anyone can stop them, it’s you.”

Rex studied her for a long moment, then folded the map and tucked it back into the bone's compartment. He closed it with a soft click, his resolve hardening. The stakes had risen, but Rex Barkley wasn't about to back down.

"Get out of here," he said, his tone brusque but not unkind. "And stay out of trouble."

The Siamese nodded, slipping back into the shadows as Rex turned his attention back to the map. The word *Dominion* loomed large in his mind, a stark reminder of the Cartel's ambitions. The city wasn't just at risk—it was on the brink of a war.

Adjusting his hat, Rex pocketed the bone and stepped into the night. The Cartel had drawn their battle lines, but Rex wasn't about to let them win without a fight.

The warehouse was alive now, the quiet broken by shouts and hurried footsteps as the Cartel realized something was amiss. Rex Barkley pressed himself against a stack of crates, his sharp ears twitching at the echo of orders being barked through the cavernous space.

"Check the offices! He couldn't have gotten far!" one voice growled, its edge sharp with authority.

"He's got the bone!" another snapped, panic lacing the words. "If he gets out with that—"

"He won't," the first voice cut in. "Find him!"

Rex clutched the bone tightly, its hidden compartment still securely sealed, and scanned the dimly lit warehouse for an escape route. His sharp eyes caught a narrow path between two towering stacks of crates leading toward the rear of the building. It wasn't ideal, but it was his best shot.

The sound of boots clattering against the concrete floor grew louder, and Rex knew he couldn't linger. He moved swiftly but silently, his paws landing with practiced precision. The adrenaline pumping through him sharpened his senses, every shadow and sound feeding his instincts.

As he reached the end of the path, the dim light shifted, and a figure emerged from the opposite direction—a burly Rottweiler with a scar running across his muzzle. The dog froze for a moment, his eyes locking onto Rex, before letting out a guttural growl.

"There you are!" the Rottweiler snarled, reaching for the knife strapped to his belt.

Rex didn't hesitate. "Sorry, pal," he muttered, grabbing a nearby crate and shoving it toward the Rottweiler. The heavy box caught him mid-lunge, knocking him back with a sharp grunt.

"Get him!" the Rottweiler roared as he stumbled, his voice carrying through the warehouse.

The commotion drew more attention. Two more figures appeared at the far end of the corridor—a Siamese and a wiry tabby, both armed with clubs. Rex cursed under his breath, his options narrowing. He turned sharply, darting toward the back of the warehouse, his boots echoing against the cold floor.

"Cut him off!" someone shouted behind him.

Rex's mind raced as he spotted a set of stairs leading to a catwalk above. He took them two at a time, the bone still clutched in one paw as the sounds of pursuit grew louder. The catwalk creaked under his weight, but he didn't stop. Below him, shadows darted between crates, the Cartel's goons scrambling to cut him off.

"Up there!" one of them shouted, pointing.

A shot rang out, the sharp crack echoing through the space as a bullet ricocheted off the metal railing inches from Rex's head. He ducked instinctively, his heart pounding as he sprinted toward a door at the far end of the catwalk. Reaching it, he yanked it open and slipped inside, slamming it shut behind him.

The room was small and dark, the faint hum of machinery vibrating through the walls. Rex leaned against the door for a moment, catching his breath as he assessed his next move. He couldn't stay here long—they'd find him soon enough.

The sound of voices outside the door made his ears twitch.

"He went this way!"

"Surround the exits! He's not getting out alive."

Rex scanned the room, his sharp eyes landing on a ventilation shaft near the ceiling. It was a tight fit, but it would have to do. He pulled a crate beneath it and climbed up, using the last of his strength to wrench the cover free before crawling inside. The metal was cold against his paws, the confined space forcing him to move slowly and deliberately.

The voices outside grew louder, and then the door burst open with a deafening crash.

"Search everywhere!" the Rottweiler barked.

Rex held his breath, his body pressed tightly against the metal as he listened to the heavy thud of boots below. They were close—too close—but he forced himself to stay still. The sound of crates being overturned and angry muttering filled the air.

"He's not here," one voice growled.

"Keep looking!" the Rottweiler snapped. "He's got to be close."

The voices began to fade as the goons moved deeper into the warehouse, but Rex didn't relax. He waited, counting each second, until the only sound left was the faint hum of machinery and his own heartbeat.

Carefully, he resumed his crawl through the shaft, following the faint draft of fresh air. After what felt like an eternity, he reached another vent cover. Peering through, he saw a narrow alley below, slick with rain and mercifully empty. With a grunt of effort, he pushed the cover loose and dropped down, landing with a soft thud.

The cool night air hit him like a shock, and for a moment, he just stood there, breathing deeply. But the sound of distant voices spurred him into motion. He adjusted his hat, clutching the bone tightly as he slipped into the shadows.

The city stretched out before him, its neon glow a stark contrast to the darkness he'd just escaped. The bone's weight felt heavier now, its hidden secrets more dangerous than ever. The Cartel wouldn't stop hunting him, not until they had it back—and Rex wasn't about to let that happen.

As he disappeared into the night, his mind churned with the implications of what he'd found. The map, the word *Dominion*, and the Cartel's ambitions painted a grim picture. The stakes weren't just personal anymore—they were citywide. And Rex Barkley wasn't about to let Barkington fall without a fight.

Chapter 13
The Cartel's Dominion

The rain battered the rooftops of Barkington, the wind howling through the cracks of forgotten buildings like a pack of restless hounds. **Rex Barkley** stood in the center of the old shipping yard, the steel skeleton of an unfinished warehouse towering above him. Pools of water collected between the rusted tracks, reflecting the cold glow of the city lights in the distance. He'd been here before—places like this, where shadows held secrets and every breath felt like it could be your last. But tonight, something was different. The air crackled with anticipation, sharp and bitter like the first bite of winter.

Across from him, **Miss Whiskers** stepped out of the dark, her silhouette framed by the eerie gleam of the streetlamp behind her. She walked slowly, deliberately, every step echoing against the empty yard. Her diamond collar caught the faint light, sparkling like a crown she hadn't claimed yet. Behind her, two of her hench-cats flanked her, eyes narrowed and claws poised, ready to pounce if Rex so much as twitched.

"You always did like dramatic meetings," Rex said, his voice low and gravelly as he pulled his coat tighter against the wind. "It suits you, Whiskers. But I'm not in the mood for games tonight."

Miss Whiskers stopped just short of him, a faint smile curling at the edges of her mouth. "Oh, but Rex, everything we've done has been part of a game. You just didn't realize you were playing until now."

Rex's eyes narrowed, every muscle in his body tense. "You led me here. Why don't you tell me what this is really about? No riddles. No purring."

She tilted her head slightly, her blue eyes gleaming with satisfaction. "Fine, hound. I'll indulge you." She took a step closer, the shadows softening against her perfectly-kept fur. "From the moment I walked into your office, you've been sniffing around the edges of a story you were never meant to understand. But you were predictable, Rex—so predictable. I knew you'd follow the trail wherever I laid it. A useful pawn in a city of broken kings."

Rex didn't flinch, though her words hit like a knife twisting under his ribs. "You used me."

Miss Whiskers let out a soft, amused laugh, like she'd heard the most obvious statement in the world. "Of course I did. Did you think you were going to save the city? Expose the Cartel? Topple the Kennel Club?" She shook her head slowly, almost pitying. "That's not how this works, Rex. Power isn't won with righteous intentions. It's taken—piece by piece, claw by claw."

"And the diamond bone?" Rex asked, his voice tight. "What's the endgame, Whiskers? You gonna throw a parade for yourself when you unlock that vault?"

Her smile sharpened into something cold and dangerous. "The vault isn't just leverage, Rex—it's **control**. With it, I'll have the Kennel Club begging at my feet and the Alley Cartel clawing to serve me. This city doesn't need peace. It needs a ruler. Someone smart enough to pull the strings. Someone who understands that power must be absolute."

Rex shook his head, his jaw tight as the realization settled over him like a wet blanket. "You've lost it. You think you're going to run this city like a queen, but you'll end up just like the rest of them—buried in the dirt when someone sharper comes along."

She took another step toward him, closing the space between them, her voice dropping to a soft, dangerous purr. "The difference between them and me, Rex? I don't make mistakes."

Rex's fists curled at his sides, his gaze burning into hers. "You made one tonight."

"Did I?" she sneered, her smile widening as she looked him over. "Tell me, Rex—what do you have left? Mittens? Lola? They're just as broken as you are. And now you're here, in the middle of a storm you can't control, standing exactly where I wanted you."

Rex's lips pulled into a faint snarl. "I'll stop you, Whiskers. I don't care how far I have to chase you."

Her laugh was soft but cruel, echoing through the empty yard. "And that's what I love about you, Rex. Always the noble bloodhound, always convinced you're the one with the truth on your side. But here's the truth you don't want to hear: You don't matter. You're just a footnote in my rise."

Her words hung there for a moment, sinking into the cold rain that splattered across the pavement. Rex's heart pounded in his chest, anger simmering just beneath the surface, but he didn't let it break him. Instead, he stepped forward, his voice low and steady.

"You might have me outnumbered, Whiskers, but you don't have me beat. You're playing a dangerous game, and sooner or later, someone's going to knock you off your throne."

Miss Whiskers' smile faltered for just a second before she masked it, her tail flicking with agitation. "Keep barking, Rex. We'll see who's left standing when the dust clears."

Rex's gaze didn't waver. "I'll be there, Whiskers. Count on it."

She stared at him for a beat longer, her expression unreadable, before turning on her heel. "Come," she ordered her crew, her voice sharp. "We're done here."

The hench-cats fell into step behind her as she disappeared into the shadows, leaving Rex alone in the rain, her words ringing in his ears. **"A useful pawn."**

For a long moment, he didn't move, the water running in rivulets down his hat, soaking through his coat. The truth was as bitter as the wind cutting through the yard. She'd played him—played him better than anyone ever had. But if she thought that was the end, she didn't know Rex Barkley.

He straightened slowly, his breath steadying. Miss Whiskers had her plan. Fine. Let her think she'd already won.

"Not yet," Rex muttered under his breath, his voice a quiet promise to himself. "Not by a long shot."

With a determined step, he turned and walked back into the night, his shadow swallowed by the rain and mist. Whatever it took—no matter the cost—he was going to bring her down.

The air inside the factory erupted into a cacophony of snarls, yells, and the crash of bodies hitting steel. **Rex Barkley** barely had time to duck as a crowbar whizzed past his head, clanging against a support beam with enough force to send sparks skittering across the floor.

"About time we stopped talking!" **Mittens Malone** shouted, his voice echoing through the cavernous space as he lunged at one of Miss Whiskers' hench-cats. His claws flashed, raking against the thug's side as they crashed into a pile of fish barrels that exploded like a tidal wave, the brine and stench spreading across the concrete.

"Watch yourself, Malone!" Rex barked, sliding under a conveyor belt just as two more cats came charging at him from the flank. His trench coat snagged on a nail, but he yanked free, rolling to his feet. One of the thugs—a muscular tabby with a scar across his eye—lunged for him, fists swinging.

Rex sidestepped, his shoulder screaming in protest, and drove an uppercut into the thug's jaw. The cat staggered back, stunned, just as Rex grabbed a loose wrench from the floor and swung it hard into the tabby's gut.

"Didn't your boss teach you not to pick fights you can't win?" Rex growled, shoving the thug into a stack of crates.

Across the room, **Lola Labrador** was holding her own, her movements sharp and efficient. She ducked low as a hench-cat swiped at her with a blade, the steel singing through the air. With a quick spin, she grabbed a length of chain hanging from a pulley and whipped it around, catching the thug's wrist and yanking him off balance.

"You boys are quick," she snapped, slamming her elbow into the cat's face, "but I'm quicker."

The cat hit the ground with a groan, and Lola stepped back, breathing hard. She glanced toward Rex, who was fending off another pair of attackers. "This is getting out of hand!"

"Yeah?" Rex shouted back, twisting to avoid a wild punch before landing a sharp jab to his opponent's chin. "Welcome to Barkington!"

Above them, the steel catwalk rattled as Miss Whiskers watched the chaos unfold with an expression that was equal parts amusement and annoyance. "Is this really the best you can do, Rex?" she called out, her voice cutting through the noise. "You're outnumbered, outmatched, and running out of time!"

Rex shot her a glare, wiping blood from his lip. "I've heard worse odds!"

Mittens, his fur slick with sweat and fish oil, leapt onto a moving conveyor belt, using the momentum to launch himself at a pair of Whiskers' goons. "Barkley!" he yelled as he collided with them, sending all three sprawling onto the factory floor. "You better have a plan, or this is gonna be my last favor!"

Rex ducked as another barrel came rolling toward him, its contents bursting open with a *wet slap* that sent fish sliding across the ground. He planted his feet and scanned the room, his mind racing. Conveyor belts sparked as they groaned under the weight of toppled crates, the overhead lights flickering as smoke began curling up from the machinery. It wouldn't take much more to turn the factory into a deathtrap.

"Lola! Malone!" Rex shouted, his voice cutting through the din. "Get to the breaker switch! Shut this place down before we all go up in flames!"

Lola's eyes darted toward the far wall where a control panel stood partially obscured by crates and debris. "On it!" she called, bolting toward the switch as Mittens fought his way back to his feet.

"I'm not taking orders from you, Barkley!" Mittens spat, swatting away a hench-cat with a clawed swipe.

"Fine," Rex growled, punching another thug square in the nose. "Pretend it's *your* idea!"

Lola vaulted over a stack of crates, sliding across a slick patch of concrete as a pair of Whiskers' thugs noticed her and moved to intercept. "Oh, no, you don't," she muttered, grabbing a discarded crowbar and swinging it low, sweeping their legs out from under them. They hit the ground hard, and Lola didn't look back as she scrambled toward the control panel.

Miss Whiskers' voice rang out again from the catwalk above, sharper this time. "Stop them, you fools! Bring me Barkley!"

Rex glanced up, locking eyes with her. She was furious now, her claws digging into the railing as she barked orders to her crew.

"You look nervous, Whiskers!" Rex shouted, dodging a wild swing and slamming his attacker into a barrel. "Not part of the plan, huh?"

"You'll regret this, Rex!" she hissed, her voice laced with venom. "When this is over, I'll have your head and the city both!"

"Get in line!" Rex shot back, darting toward the conveyor belt. He grabbed a loose gear from the floor and hurled it like a discus, striking one of the guards square in the back. The thug crumpled, groaning, just as a loud *bang* echoed from across the room.

"Got it!" Lola shouted as she slammed her paw into the breaker switch.

The factory shuddered as the lights flickered wildly before dying out with a heavy *thunk*. The machinery groaned one last time before the belts ground to a halt, leaving the room lit only by the flickering glow of a single emergency light. Smoke billowed in the dimness, and the remaining hench-cats hesitated, their confidence rattled.

Miss Whiskers' silhouette loomed on the catwalk, her tail flicking in frustration. "This isn't over, Barkley!" she snarled. "You've only delayed the inevitable!"

Rex wiped a hand across his face, his breath coming in sharp bursts. "You'd better run, Whiskers. Because next time, you won't get away."

Her glare burned down at him, but she didn't answer. With a flick of her paw, she turned and disappeared into the shadows, her remaining crew scattering like rats.

As the factory fell silent except for the creak of settling metal, Rex, Lola, and Mittens stood there, bruised and breathless.

"You call that a plan?" Mittens muttered, his fur disheveled.

"Better than nothing," Rex replied, adjusting his hat. He glanced toward the catwalk where Whiskers had been moments ago, his jaw tightening. "She's slipping away, but not for long. She wants the vault. She's not getting it."

Lola nodded, her voice steady despite the chaos. "Then we end this. Once and for all."

Rex stared into the dark, his voice low. "Yeah. One way or another, this ends tonight."

The factory floor was a battlefield of shadows and smoke, the air still humming with the chaos Miss Whiskers had left in her wake. **Rex Barkley** stood in the middle of it all, breathing hard, his trench coat streaked with grime and blood. Across the room, **Lola Labrador** and **Mittens Malone** were regrouping, their eyes darting toward him, waiting for his next move.

But Rex wasn't looking at them. His gaze stayed fixed on the catwalk above, where Miss Whiskers had retreated just minutes before. He knew she'd be back. Someone like her didn't slink into the dark without a plan, and Rex had learned long ago that you never let a predator out of your sight—not until you knew where their claws were headed.

The faint sound of footsteps echoed through the rafters. Then she appeared again, emerging from the shadows with her fur sleek and pristine, her diamond collar glinting under the emergency light. Her expression, however, was no longer calm and collected. Her icy demeanor had cracked just enough for him to see the fury burning beneath.

"Barkley," Miss Whiskers purred, though her voice carried a tremor of restraint. "I'm getting tired of this game."

Rex smirked, his bruised jaw aching. "You're the one who started it, Whiskers. You don't get to quit now."

She descended the metal staircase slowly, her claws clicking against the steps with deliberate menace. Her hench-cats gathered again in the periphery, waiting for her signal. The factory had quieted, but the tension hung in the air like a blade dangling by a thread.

"You think you've won something here tonight?" she sneered, stopping a few feet away from Rex. "You've delayed me, *humiliated* me in front of my crew, but let me remind you—*I* hold the cards. You're just a dog who doesn't know when to stop barking."

Rex held her gaze, unflinching. "You've got a problem, Whiskers. You assume the rest of us are playing by your rules."

She tilted her head, her smile returning. "What are you talking about, Rex? You're cornered, outnumbered, and still clinging to whatever shred of pride you have left. The bone is mine. And when I open that vault, you'll wish you'd stayed in your office where you belonged."

Rex let the words hang for a beat, his silence baiting her. Then, slowly, he reached into his coat pocket. The room tensed as her hench-cats shifted, watching him like a pack ready to pounce.

"I've got bad news for you," Rex said finally, pulling out the **bone**—or at least, something that looked like it. It gleamed under the flickering factory light, the diamond studs catching every shadow. Miss Whiskers' eyes locked onto it, her confidence flaring again like a flame reignited.

"You're full of tricks, Barkley," she purred, stepping closer. "But now you're holding something you can't bluff your way out of."

Rex's grip on the bone tightened, his voice steady. "Funny thing about trust, Whiskers. You broke mine the moment you stepped into my office. So I figured it was time to return the favor."

Her smile faltered. "What are you—"

Rex tossed the bone into the air. For the briefest moment, the entire room froze. The object spun lazily, light dancing across its surface, and Miss Whiskers' eyes widened as she reached out, her claws snapping to grab it mid-air. The bone landed in her paw, and her grip closed around it like a vice. She stared at it for half a beat, her triumphant smirk creeping back.

And then the smirk faltered.

Her claws turned the bone over once, then again, her face falling into confusion as realization set in. "What... what is this?"

Rex crossed his arms, his voice dripping with satisfaction. "A decoy. Pretty good work, huh? A little paint, a few cheap stones, and you've got yourself something that looks the part."

Miss Whiskers' fur bristled, her tail snapping like a whip. "You *swapped it?*" Her voice rose, shrill with anger as she hurled the fake bone to the ground. It clattered across the concrete, hollow and worthless.

"Thought you were smarter than me, didn't you?" Rex continued, his expression calm despite the chaos swirling around them. "You were so sure you had the bone—so sure you'd already won—that you didn't stop to question how easy it all was."

"Where is it?" she hissed, her composure crumbling, her claws flexing at her sides.

"Not where you can get your paws on it," Rex replied. "And certainly not where you're going to open that vault tonight."

Her hench-cats stirred anxiously, exchanging uncertain glances as they watched their boss unravel. Miss Whiskers shot them a glare, her voice lashing out like a whip. "What are you waiting for? *Get him!*"

"Too late for that," a voice rang out from the dark.

Miss Whiskers' head snapped toward the sound as **Lola Labrador** and **Mittens Malone** emerged from the shadows behind her crew, their expressions sharp, their claws—and fists—ready.

"This is over, Whiskers," Lola said firmly, stepping forward.

Mittens grinned faintly, his teeth glinting. "Told you not to underestimate us, didn't I?"

Chaos erupted again as Whiskers' hench-cats spun to face the new threat. Mittens and Lola descended like a storm, fists flying and claws slashing as they cut through her crew with practiced precision.

Miss Whiskers turned back to Rex, her eyes wild with fury. "You think this is over, Barkley? You think you've won?"

Rex's voice was calm, steady as ever. "I think you've lost the upper paw. And I think it's time you realized that."

Her breath came in short bursts as her crew crumbled around her, the sounds of bodies hitting the ground echoing through the factory. With a snarl, she turned and bolted toward the far exit, disappearing into the shadows before Rex could stop her.

Rex watched her go, his chest heaving as he adjusted the brim of his hat. "She's not going far," he muttered to himself. "Not this time."

Lola stepped up beside him, wiping blood from her knuckles. "She's desperate. That's when they make mistakes."

Mittens appeared on his other side, breathing hard. "You'd better hope you've got a real plan, Barkley. Because she's not giving up."

Rex nodded, his eyes fixed on the darkness where Miss Whiskers had disappeared. "Neither are we."

The factory fell silent, save for the faint hum of dying machinery and the rain still tapping against the broken windows. Whatever Whiskers had planned, whatever game she was still playing, Rex knew one thing: this wasn't over. Not yet.

Chapter 14
The Stage of Lies

The rain pounded relentlessly as Rex Barkley pushed through the door of the abandoned vault room, his coat slicked against his frame and his hat pulled low to shield his face. The building—a forgotten warehouse nestled in the deepest part of Barkington's dockyards—loomed like a sleeping beast, its silence unnerving after the chaos he'd left behind.

In his paw, he gripped the **real diamond bone**. The weight of it felt heavier than it should've been, like the entire city of Barkington was pressing down on it. The bone gleamed faintly under the dull emergency lights, its diamond studs catching reflections like sharp glints of teeth. **Lola Labrador** and **Mittens Malone** flanked him, their breaths audible in the cold air as they surveyed the cavernous space.

"You sure about this, Barkley?" Mittens muttered, his claws flexing restlessly. His yellow eyes darted to the vault's steel door looming at the far end of the room, larger and more foreboding now than it had been in their imaginations. "Once you open that thing, there's no going back."

"Hasn't been any going back since the night Whiskers walked into my office," Rex replied, his voice gravelly and low. "We've come this far. We finish it."

Lola stepped forward, her sharp amber eyes locked on the vault door. "Let's hope what's inside is worth it. You really think this changes anything, Rex?"

"It changes everything," Rex said, moving toward the vault. His voice carried an edge of finality that settled over the room like a fog. "It's proof—names, dates, payouts. The whole rotten structure laid bare for anyone willing to see it. Once this opens, Whiskers won't be the only one looking over her shoulder."

Mittens snorted faintly. "You think proof's gonna matter to dogs like the Kennel Club? Or to the Cartel? They'll bury it, Barkley. And they'll bury us right along with it."

Rex didn't answer. Instead, he stopped before the vault door, the faint hum of its mechanisms vibrating through the floor. The pawprint scanner glowed dimly, waiting—expecting—the key that would unlock what lay inside.

Rex held up the bone, turning it once in his grip. For all its brilliance, the thing was ugly now, tainted by the greed, corruption, and betrayal that had swirled around it. His gaze flickered to Lola and Mittens. "You two ready for this?"

Lola exhaled softly, her voice steady. "Ready or not, we're here."

Mittens flicked his tail, his usual sarcasm muted. "Just don't screw it up, Barkley. I didn't come this far for nothing."

Rex nodded once and turned back to the scanner. Carefully, he placed the bone against the glowing panel, the studded diamonds aligning with the etched pawprint carved into the steel. For a moment, nothing happened. Then the scanner let out a faint *beep*, and the ground seemed to shudder as unseen gears began grinding into motion.

The lights in the room dimmed as the vault door groaned, a deep rumble echoing off the walls. Slowly, it began to slide open, releasing a gust of stale, cold air that carried the weight of secrets long buried. Mittens muttered a curse under his breath, and Lola's eyes narrowed as they waited for the door to fully reveal its contents.

When the grinding finally stopped, the room fell silent again, save for the rhythmic drip of water somewhere in the distance.

Rex stepped forward first, the beam of his flashlight cutting through the darkness beyond the vault door. The space inside was vast, lined with rows of filing cabinets, locked safes, and shelves stacked high with manila folders, ledgers, and records that stretched back decades. Each one, Rex knew, was a weapon—evidence of the schemes and secrets that had kept Barkington under the thumb of the Kennel Club and the Alley Cartel for years.

"Mother of bones," Mittens whispered as he stepped in after Rex. "She wasn't kidding. It's all here."

Lola picked up a ledger from one of the shelves, flipping through the crisp pages. "Payouts to city officials, bribes for police, contracts for smuggling routes… Names everywhere. It's worse than we thought."

Rex scanned the room, his expression dark as he pieced it together. "This is the heart of it all. Every deal, every crime, every secret tied to the Kennel Club and the Cartel—it's all been documented. Whoever controls this vault doesn't just hold power. They *own* the city."

Lola looked at him, her voice cautious. "And what happens now, Rex? This doesn't end with the vault opening. It just starts another war."

Rex didn't answer right away. He reached for a thick file at the center of a metal desk and opened it, his eyes narrowing at the contents. There, under crisp headers and red ink, were names he recognized—**Commissioner Bowser**, high-ranking Cartel lieutenants, even the heads of Barkington's richest families. All of them had been bought, all of them pawns in a larger game.

"This isn't just about the bone," Rex muttered, his voice cold. "Whiskers didn't want this for leverage. She wanted this to burn the Kennel Club to the ground and build her own empire on the ashes."

Mittens barked out a bitter laugh. "She almost pulled it off. If you hadn't swapped that bone, she'd be sitting in here right now, holding the leash."

"And the rest of us would be dancing to her tune," Lola added grimly, shutting the ledger in her paw.

Rex's jaw tightened as he turned to face them. "This changes everything. We don't just stop Whiskers. We end this—once and for all."

Mittens stared at him, suspicion flickering in his eyes. "And how exactly do you plan on doing that, Barkley? Taking this to the papers? The cops? You think they'll listen?"

"They'll have to," Rex said, holding up the file. "If we can make this public—really public—then no one gets to bury it. Not the Cartel. Not the Kennel Club. Not even Whiskers."

Lola stepped closer, her voice cautious but resolute. "It won't be easy, Rex. Everyone in this city will want us dead for what's in this vault."

"Good," Rex replied, his voice dark as he turned back to the open door. "That means we're finally on the right trail."

The hum of the vault lingered as they stood there, surrounded by the weight of Barkington's sins. For the first time in a long time, Rex felt like he was holding something real—something that could turn the tide. But he also knew the cost.

If Miss Whiskers wanted war, she was about to get one. And Rex Barkley was ready to fight.

The vault's open maw loomed behind Rex Barkley, its dark depths lined with files and ledgers that could burn the whole city to the ground. But it wasn't the vault or the secrets inside that held his focus now. It was **Miss Whiskers**, stepping out of the shadows with a feline grace that bordered on unnatural, her blue eyes glinting with a menace he'd underestimated until now.

Her presence alone made the room colder, as though the air itself had started recoiling from her. Behind her, her loyal hench-cats prowled in silent formation, but Rex's gut told him it wasn't the muscle he needed to worry about. It was her **Whiskerweaving.**

"Barkley," Miss Whiskers purred, her voice smooth but edged with venom. "You really do have a knack for surviving. It's almost impressive."

Rex tightened his grip on his revolver, the barrel glinting under the flickering warehouse lights. Beside him, **Mittens Malone** crouched low, his claws flexing in and out, his eyes flicking to Whiskers' every move.

"You're cornered, Whiskers," Rex said, his voice steady. "This ends here."

She tilted her head, the smile on her face widening into something cruel. "Cornered? Oh, Rex. You're still playing the wrong game. Do you think this is about brute strength? About bullets and claws?"

Rex didn't answer. His instincts told him to move, to act—but something about the way she held herself, unshaken and unbothered, sent a warning through his veins.

"I tried giving you a way out," Whiskers continued, her tone softening as she took a measured step forward. "But you just couldn't resist sniffing where you didn't belong."

And then her eyes narrowed, her whiskers twitching with a subtle flick. The air shimmered.

"Rex," Mittens growled under his breath. "She's—"

Before he could finish, the room twisted. The vault's walls stretched and contorted as if the entire space had been pulled through a looking glass. The air wavered with strange energy, and suddenly the concrete floor beneath them was no longer solid. Rex staggered, his vision swimming as phantom shapes bloomed around him—dark silhouettes flickering like shadows thrown against candlelight.

"Illusions."

The realization hit him like a slap. Miss Whiskers' **Whiskerweaving** magic was as dangerous as it was deceptive. Around him, the figures sharpened into form: snarling hounds with glowing red eyes, their jaws dripping shadow like oil, circling him with low, guttural growls. Somewhere in the shifting darkness, he could hear Whiskers' voice, taunting and echoing from every direction.

"You wanted a fight, Barkley. Let's see how well you do when you can't tell what's real."

Rex shook his head, forcing himself to focus, his breathing controlled despite the rising dread clawing at his throat. The illusions were vivid, alive, but they weren't solid. Whiskers was trying to trap him in his own head.

"Rex!" Mittens' voice cut through, sharp and urgent. The tabby swiped at one of the phantom hounds, his claws passing through it harmlessly before it dissolved into smoke and reformed elsewhere. "They're everywhere!"

"They're *nothing!*" Rex barked, his voice loud and deliberate. He forced his boots into the floor, steadying himself. "Keep moving! She's trying to disorient us!"

Miss Whiskers' laughter rang through the room, cold and distant. "You can't fight what you can't see, Rex. And you can't win when the ground shifts beneath your feet."

The vault's glow pulsed unnaturally, and suddenly one of the shadowy illusions lunged at Rex, its jaws wide and snarling. Rex rolled to the side, his revolver snapping up and firing—only for the bullet to rip through the figure harmlessly. The hound exploded into smoke, reforming seconds later on his flank.

"Damn it," Rex muttered, wiping sweat from his brow as his gaze darted around. It was like trying to fight smoke with fists. He needed something else. Something sharper.

Then he remembered: **Pawglyphs.**

Years ago, he'd stumbled onto the faint art of those strange symbols, scraps of knowledge left behind by the old-world hounds who knew how to disrupt magic like Whiskers'. He didn't trust it then, and he barely trusted it now. But it was all he had.

"Keep her busy!" Rex shouted to Mittens, who was fending off yet another illusion.

"What do you think I'm doing?!" Mittens snapped back, his voice tight as he clawed at empty air.

Rex dropped to one knee and dragged his paw through the dirt-streaked concrete, drawing out a series of lines—jagged and deliberate, like broken claw marks—until the faint shape of a **Pawglyph** emerged. It wasn't elegant, but it didn't need to be. The moment he completed it, the air around him hummed sharply, a pulse of energy rippling outward.

The closest shadow hound shrieked, its form warping and scattering like smoke caught in a gale.

Miss Whiskers' voice snapped, her calm breaking. "What are you doing, Barkley?"

"Evening the odds," Rex muttered. He wiped the grime off his paw and drew another quick glyph, his breath coming faster now. The illusions flickered violently, several of them splitting apart, their forms unraveling as though Whiskers' hold was slipping.

Mittens staggered over to him, his chest heaving. "Whatever you're doing, keep it up!"

Rex nodded, his focus razor-sharp. He stood and locked eyes on the last place Whiskers' voice had echoed from. "Your tricks aren't working, Whiskers. You're running out of time."

There was silence for a beat, and then her voice, soft but furious: "You don't understand what you're undoing, Rex. You think this city will thank you for this? You're just dragging it into the dark."

Rex's lip curled into a smirk, the last of the illusions finally dissolving as the Pawglyphs cut through her magic. "No, Whiskers. I'm dragging *you* into the light."

The air stilled, and for the first time, the factory was silent again—no echoes, no tricks. Somewhere in the dark, Rex knew she was still there, retreating but not defeated.

"Let's end this," Rex said, adjusting his hat as Mittens and Lola regrouped beside him. "She's running scared now. We push forward, we take her down, and we put this city back together."

As the echoes of Whiskers' illusions faded into nothing, the real fight was just beginning.

The factory groaned like a wounded beast as the last remnants of **Miss Whiskers' illusions** dissipated into the shadows. The air was thick, still buzzing faintly from the Pawglyphs Rex

Barkley had etched into the concrete moments before. The shadows settled back into their corners, leaving behind only the three of them—**Rex, Mittens Malone, and Lola Labrador**—standing amidst the wreckage.

The vault yawned behind them, its secrets laid bare. Papers and ledgers were scattered across the floor, the truth finally dragged into the light. But Rex barely had time to register the victory before a quiet sound—like silk brushing against steel—pricked his ears.

"Where is she?" Lola muttered, turning sharply, her eyes darting to every corner of the vast room.

"She's not done," Mittens growled, his fur bristling. "She wouldn't run without trying to claw something back."

Rex didn't respond. His grip tightened on his revolver as he scanned the darkened rafters and the maze of catwalks overhead. Miss Whiskers was still out there, hidden somewhere in the factory's skeletal shadows, watching them, waiting.

A faint voice—soft, but sharp as a knife—echoed from above.

"Congratulations, Barkley. You've won the battle."

Rex turned toward the sound, his eyes narrowing as Miss Whiskers stepped into the faint light filtering through a shattered window. She stood on a rusted catwalk, her silhouette sleek and composed despite everything she'd lost. Her diamond collar caught the dim glow, a glint of pride still unshaken.

"But you haven't won the war," she continued, her voice smooth but laced with venom. "Do you think dragging my plans into the light will fix this city? Barkington isn't built on truth, Rex—it's built on power. And power always finds a way."

"Save the speeches, Whiskers," Rex called back, his voice gravelly but steady. "Your plans are in shreds, and the vault's open. The Kennel Club, the Cartel—they're all going to see what you were trying to pull. You're done."

She laughed softly, the sound echoing hollow against the metal walls. "You're still so naive, Rex. Do you really think the truth changes anything? You'll scatter the rats for a while, but they'll come crawling back. They always do. You're holding evidence, sure—but evidence is only as strong as the hands holding it."

Rex raised his revolver, leveling it toward her. "We'll see about that."

Her eyes flashed, the blue gleam hard as steel. "You won't pull that trigger, Rex. You're too righteous for that. It's why you're standing there, holding your scraps of victory, while I walk away."

"She's bluffing," Mittens snarled, his claws flexing. "Shoot her and be done with it!"

"Rex, don't let her slip away," Lola urged, her voice tight.

Rex didn't move. His paw stayed steady, finger poised on the trigger. But her words hung there, sharp and deliberate, weaving their way into the air. She knew him too well—knew he wasn't the type to shoot a fleeing enemy in the back, even if that enemy had put him through hell.

"You don't want me dead, Rex," she said softly, her tone almost coaxing now. "Not really. You need me out there, don't you? Someone to chase. Someone to keep you sharp."

Rex's jaw tightened. "I'm not playing your games anymore, Whiskers."

She smiled faintly. "Oh, but you will. Because you can't help yourself."

Before he could react, she moved. Her paw darted toward the chain beside her, and with a sharp tug, the catwalk's emergency escape ladder dropped with a metallic *clang*. She leapt onto it with grace only a cat could manage, disappearing down into the shadows before Rex could fire.

"Damn it!" Rex shouted, the revolver lowering as her figure melted into the dark.

Mittens snarled in frustration. "She's running, Barkley! We can't let her get away!"

"Save it!" Rex barked back, his voice echoing through the empty space. "She's gone."

Lola exhaled sharply, her shoulders slumping as she turned toward him. "We had her, Rex. We could've ended this."

Rex shoved his revolver back into his coat, his jaw set in frustration. "We ended enough tonight."

He turned toward the vault, its secrets scattered like broken glass across the floor. Ledgers, contracts, payouts—all of it tied back to the Kennel Club and the Alley Cartel. All of it enough to scorch the city's rotten foundations.

"It's over," Rex said quietly, though the words tasted bitter on his tongue. "Her plan's shot, and now we've got the truth."

Mittens shook his head, his voice low and biting. "You call this a win? She's still out there, Barkley. Mark my words—she'll claw her way back."

"Let her try," Rex replied, turning to face him. His expression was hard, his eyes carrying the weight of everything they'd fought for. "She's not getting another chance. Not with this."

He gestured to the vault, to the stacks of evidence that could bring down the city's biggest players. It wasn't clean, and it wasn't final, but it was enough.

Lola stepped up beside him, her voice soft. "So what now, Rex? We've got the proof—but where do we take it?"

Rex adjusted the brim of his hat, his gaze fixed on the darkened doorway where Whiskers had disappeared. "We don't stop moving, that's what. The truth's out. Now we make sure no one buries it."

Mittens scoffed faintly, but his tone lacked its usual venom. "You're playing a dangerous game, Barkley."

Rex smirked faintly, though there was no humor behind it. "Yeah. But it's the only game I know how to play."

The three of them stood in silence for a moment, the hum of the factory fading into the sound of the rain drumming against the windows. Miss Whiskers had escaped into the night, but the diamond bone and the vault were no longer hers to claim. It was a victory, but Rex could feel the cost settling deep in his bones.

"Come on," he said finally, turning toward the exit. "We've got work to do."

As they stepped out into the rain, the factory behind them felt heavy with unfinished business. Miss Whiskers had lost tonight—but she wasn't gone. Not yet. And Rex knew the next time they crossed paths, one of them wouldn't be walking away.

Chapter 15
Shattered Bonds

The rain hammered against the skylights of the abandoned theater, the sound reverberating through the cavernous space like a heartbeat. Rex Barkley stood at the center of the stage, the weight of the diamond-encrusted bone in his paw heavier than it had ever been. His sharp eyes shifted between the two figures standing on opposite ends of the room: Miss Whiskers, poised and calm as ever, and Mittens Malone, his sharp claws glinting in the faint light.

"Well, isn't this cozy?" Rex said, his voice cutting through the tension. "All the key players under one roof. Saves me the trouble of rounding you up."

Miss Whiskers' tail flicked once, a subtle betrayal of her otherwise composed demeanor. "You're awfully dramatic, Detective," she purred. "You act like you've uncovered something new."

"Maybe I have," Rex replied, his tone edged with steel. He turned his gaze to Mittens. "And you, Mittens—still skulking around in the shadows, nursing that grudge? Or are you finally ready to tell the truth?"

Mittens' golden eyes narrowed, his lips curling into a snarl. "Watch it, Barkley. I've had about enough of your mouth."

"Yeah? Well, you're gonna hear a lot more before this is over," Rex shot back. He took a deliberate step forward, his voice rising. "You both think you're smarter than everyone else, pulling strings, playing games. But the truth is, you're just two sides of the same coin—greedy, manipulative, and willing to burn this city to the ground to get what you want."

Miss Whiskers let out a soft chuckle, her blue eyes gleaming. "You always did have a flair for the dramatic. But I'm curious, Detective—what exactly do you think you've figured out?"

Rex smirked, pulling the bone from his coat and holding it up for both of them to see. "This isn't just some flashy heirloom. It's a key, a map, and a weapon all rolled into one. The Cartel's been using it to keep their power locked up tight, but you, Whiskers—you had other plans."

Miss Whiskers arched a brow, but said nothing.

"You stole the bone," Rex continued, his voice steady. "Staged the robbery to make it look like the Cartel's move, then dangled just enough clues to get me sniffing around. All so you could take the Cartel down from the inside."

Mittens let out a bitter laugh, shaking his head. "You think she's some kind of hero? Don't make me laugh. Whiskers doesn't care about this city. She just wants to wear the crown herself."

"Oh, and you're any better?" Rex shot back. "You've been clinging to the Cartel's scraps for years, waiting for a chance to crawl back to the top."

Mittens growled, his claws flexing. "Watch your tongue, hound."

"Or what?" Rex barked, his patience wearing thin. "You'll try to silence me? Go ahead, Mittens. Try it. But before you do, maybe you should think about how deep you're already in."

Miss Whiskers stepped forward, her voice cool and measured. "And what about you, Rex? You've uncovered so much. But what are you going to do with it?"

"I'll tell you what I'm not going to do," Rex said, turning to face her. "I'm not going to let either of you walk away with the bone. The Cartel's done enough damage to this city, and your little crusade isn't any better."

Her composure cracked, just slightly, her tail stilling. "You think I'm just like them?"

"I think you're worse," Rex said bluntly. "At least the Cartel doesn't pretend to be something they're not."

Mittens stepped closer, his voice low and dangerous. "And what's your plan, Barkley? You gonna play the hero? Save the city all by yourself?"

"I don't need to save the city," Rex replied, his voice steady. "I just need to make sure neither of you gets what you want."

The tension in the room was electric, the three of them standing at the center of a storm neither could fully control.

Finally, Miss Whiskers let out a soft sigh, her expression unreadable.

"You're right about one thing, Detective," she said, her voice quieter now. "The bone is dangerous. But so is letting the Cartel keep their grip on this city."

"And you think you're the one to break it?" Rex asked, his tone skeptical. "You've already proven you're willing to burn everything to get what you want."

"So what now?" Mittens growled, his sharp teeth glinting in the faint light. "You gonna destroy the bone? Hand it over to the cops?"

Rex glanced between them, the weight of the decision pressing down on him. Slowly, deliberately, he turned the bone over in his paw, his claws brushing against its intricate carvings. "No," he said finally. "I'm gonna make sure this never falls into anyone's hands again."

Before either of them could react, Rex hurled the bone against the concrete floor. The sound of shattering crystal echoed through the room as the bone splintered into countless pieces, its secrets scattered beyond repair.

Miss Whiskers stared at the fragments, her eyes wide with a mixture of shock and disbelief. "You fool," she whispered. "Do you have any idea what you've done?"

"I know exactly what I've done," Rex replied, his voice steady. "I've leveled the playing field."

Mittens snarled, his fur bristling. "You think this changes anything? The Cartel won't stop just because the bone's gone."

"Maybe not," Rex said, his gaze hard. "But now they'll be too busy cleaning up their mess to keep tearing this city apart."

The silence that followed was deafening, the weight of Rex's decision hanging heavy in the air. Without another word, he turned and walked away, leaving Miss Whiskers and Mittens to stand among the ruins of their ambitions.

The rain had started again by the time Rex stepped outside, the cold droplets washing away the night's tension. The city stretched out before him, battered but unbroken. And for the first time in a long time, Rex Barkley felt like he'd done something that mattered.

The shattered remains of the diamond-encrusted bone lay scattered across the stage, glinting faintly under the dim light. Rex Barkley stood at the center of it all, his sharp eyes flicking between the stunned figures of Miss Whiskers and Mittens Malone. The storm outside continued to rage, thunder rumbling like the city itself was holding its breath.

"You always were full of surprises, Detective," Miss Whiskers said at last, her voice carefully controlled. But her tail twitched, betraying the tension simmering just beneath her poised facade.

"I'd say the same about you," Rex replied, stepping over the fragments of the bone. He held up a small, crumpled piece of paper he'd retrieved from the hidden compartment moments before the bone was destroyed. "But I've got to admit, I didn't see this one coming."

"What is that?" Mittens growled, his golden eyes narrowing as he took a step closer. "Another one of her tricks?"

Miss Whiskers didn't flinch, but her silence was damning. Rex unfolded the paper, his claws brushing against the faded ink. The faint outlines of names, dates, and numbers spread across the page—a ledger, meticulously detailed, documenting years of criminal deals. At the top of the list was the Cartel's symbol, flanked by an unmistakable signature: **Miss Whiskers.**

"So, this is what it was all about," Rex said, his voice steady but sharp. "A ledger. Not just a fancy chew toy, but a record of every dirty deal, every payoff, every bit of leverage the Cartel's ever held. And you, Whiskers—you're right at the center of it."

Miss Whiskers finally moved, her blue eyes locking onto Rex's. "It's not what you think," she said, her voice calm but edged with something that sounded like desperation. "That ledger isn't just the Cartel's—it's a roadmap. A way to dismantle their entire operation."

Mittens let out a bitter laugh, shaking his head. "You've got some nerve, Whiskers. Trying to spin this like you're the hero. You've been in bed with the Cartel for years."

"And you haven't?" she shot back, her composure cracking as she turned on him. "Don't act like you're innocent, Mittens. We both know you've made your share of deals to stay on top."

"I never sold out the city," Mittens growled, his claws flexing. "You? You've been playing both sides, and now it's all catching up to you."

Rex stepped between them, his paw raised to cut off the brewing argument. "Enough," he barked. "I don't care how many deals you've made or who's betrayed who. What matters is what happens now."

Miss Whiskers took a step forward, her voice softening. "Rex, you have to understand. I took the ledger to protect myself— but also to use it against them. The Cartel's power is built on secrets, and that ledger exposes them all. I wasn't trying to save myself. I was trying to end them."

"And you didn't think to mention that before?" Rex asked, his tone flat.

"Would you have believed me?" she countered, her blue eyes piercing. "Everything I've done, I've done to protect this city. You've seen what the Cartel is capable of. Without that ledger, they'll keep controlling everything—every district, every deal, every life."

Mittens sneered, his tail lashing. "Don't buy into her act, Barkley. She's just looking out for herself. Always has, always will."

Rex glanced between them, his instincts buzzing. Miss Whiskers' words rang true, but so did Mittens' accusations. The ledger was damning, but it also held the key to dismantling the Cartel's empire. The question was whether Miss Whiskers could be trusted to use it—or if she'd just replace one form of control with another.

"You think destroying the bone solves anything?" Miss Whiskers asked, her voice rising. "The ledger is the only thing keeping the Cartel in check. Without it, they'll go underground, rebuild, and come back stronger."

"And you think you're the one to stop them?" Rex countered. "You've lied, manipulated, and played every angle. How am I supposed to trust you now?"

She hesitated, her gaze dropping for the briefest moment. "You don't have to trust me," she said finally. "But you know as well as I do that if the Cartel wins, this city is finished."

Mittens stepped closer, his voice low and dangerous. "She's right about one thing, Barkley. The Cartel doesn't stop. But that doesn't mean she gets to walk away with that ledger."

Rex held up the crumpled paper, his sharp eyes narrowing. "Neither of you gets to walk away with it. This ends tonight."

Miss Whiskers' eyes widened. "Rex—"

"No," he cut in, his voice firm. "You both had your chance to do the right thing, and you both blew it. The Cartel's reign ends here, and it doesn't end with either of you calling the shots."

The silence that followed was thick, the tension almost unbearable. Finally, Rex folded the paper and slipped it into his coat. "I'm taking this to the one place you can't touch it. And when the dust settles, maybe this city will finally get a chance to breathe."

Mittens snarled, his claws scraping against the floor. "You think this is over, Barkley? You don't know the Cartel. They'll come for you."

"Let them," Rex said, turning toward the exit. "I'll be waiting."

As he walked away, the weight of the ledger pressed against his chest like a ticking bomb. The rain outside hit him like a wall, cold and relentless, but Rex didn't stop. The truth had come to light, and with it, the city's darkest secrets. The game was over, but the war was just beginning.

The rain was relentless, washing the city clean in a way Rex Barkley knew wasn't meant for him. The streets glistened under the flickering streetlights, their reflections jagged and distorted, much like the case that had just come to a close. Rex leaned against a lamppost, his coat heavy with water and his ribs aching from the night's encounters. The crumpled ledger rested inside his pocket, a tangible weight that mirrored the one in his chest.

He lit a cigarette, the brief flare of the lighter cutting through the darkness. The first drag burned in a way that felt grounding, a reminder that he was still standing—bruised, battered, but alive. The theater behind him loomed like a shadow, its secrets exposed, its players scattered. Miss Whiskers had disappeared into the night, her elegance shattered but her resolve still intact. Mittens Malone had left in a snarl of anger, his claws promising retribution that Rex wouldn't lose sleep over.

As the rain traced patterns down his face, Rex couldn't stop the replay of their final words.

"You think you're any different, Barkley?" Mittens had spat, his voice echoing off the empty stage. "You act like you're above it all, but you're just like the rest of us—chasing power, chasing control."

"I'm not chasing anything," Rex had replied, his tone low and firm. "I'm just making sure neither of you burns this city down in the process."

It was true, or at least mostly true. Rex had never cared for power, but control? That was another story. Control over the truth, over the lies, over the fragile line between justice and survival—that's what kept him in the game, no matter how much it cost him.

"You're a fool, Detective," Miss Whiskers had said before vanishing into the shadows. "You think tearing it all down will save anyone? You'll see. The city will only rebuild its monsters."

Maybe she was right. The Cartel would regroup, its many heads shifting and morphing but never truly disappearing. Miss Whiskers would survive, her schemes adapting to whatever the next opportunity might be. And Mittens? He'd keep nursing his grudge until it consumed him. But that didn't mean Rex had made the wrong call. Some battles weren't about winning— they were about keeping the playing field from tilting too far in the wrong direction.

Rex exhaled a stream of smoke, his sharp eyes scanning the street. Somewhere in the distance, the faint wail of a police siren cut through the night, a reminder that the city's clockwork continued, even now.

The case was over, but what had it really solved? The bone was gone, shattered into irrelevance. The ledger—an artifact of power and corruption—was in Rex's possession, but he knew better than to believe it was a silver bullet. It would go to someone he trusted, someone who could use it without succumbing to the very temptations it cataloged. But even then, would it be enough?

His mind flicked back to the first night Miss Whiskers had walked into his office, her fur sleek and her voice smooth as velvet. She had spun a tale of loss and desperation, baiting him with the allure of a case that had felt straightforward at the time.

But nothing about this had been simple. Every thread he'd pulled had revealed another layer, each one darker than the last.

"This city's got a way of pulling you under," he muttered to himself, the words disappearing into the rain.

Had he changed? Rex wasn't sure. He was still the same dog, still chasing the truth no matter how sharp its edges. But something about this case lingered in his chest—a new kind of weight, heavier than the ledger. He'd seen the depth of ambition, the way it corroded even the sharpest minds and the purest intentions. And yet, he'd also seen the flicker of something else: the faint hope that even in a city as dark as Barkington, there were lines that could still be drawn.

He dropped the cigarette to the ground, crushing it under his heel before stepping back into the rain. The city stretched out before him, its lights fragmented and beautiful, its edges sharp as glass. There were more cases waiting, more shadows to chase, more truths to unravel. Rex adjusted his hat, his jaw tightening as he started down the street.

"Same old city," he muttered. "Same old me."

But for the first time in a long while, Rex felt something stir— a quiet resolve, a faint but steady conviction that maybe, just maybe, chasing the truth wasn't just about survival. Maybe it was about something more.

The rain fell harder, but Rex didn't quicken his pace. The city could wait. For now, it was enough to walk through its streets, a hound on the hunt, forever chasing the dawn.

Epilogue
A Hound's Resolve

The rain outside had finally subsided, leaving the streets of Barkington City slick and shimmering under the faint glow of streetlamps. Rex Barkley leaned against the threshold of his office, staring at the quiet cityscape with a cigarette dangling loosely from his lips. He had won, in some sense. The bone was destroyed, the Cartel weakened, and Miss Whiskers' plans unraveled. But victory in Barkington never felt clean. It wasn't a ribbon-cutting; it was a survival act, and the scars it left were permanent.

His reflection in the rain-dappled window stared back at him— rumpled trench coat, battered fedora, and eyes that had seen more of Barkington's darkness than most would ever dare. Rex wasn't the type to ruminate, but tonight felt different. Something in the stillness held him captive, as if the city itself wanted him to stop and take stock of what had happened.

The soft creak of the office door behind him pulled him from his thoughts. Turning slightly, Rex saw Sniffles McGruff step cautiously inside, his small frame almost swallowed by the oversized trench coat he insisted on wearing.

"You still brooding, Rex?" Sniffles asked, his voice tentative but curious. "Thought you'd be celebrating or something."

Rex chuckled, a low, gravelly sound. "Celebrating what, Sniffles? A city that's still gonna chew itself up and spit out anyone too slow to get out of the way?"

Sniffles shuffled awkwardly, then shrugged. "I mean, you did good, right? You stopped the Cartel, took the bone out of the game. That's something."

"Maybe," Rex said, exhaling a cloud of smoke. "But it doesn't change what this place is. Doesn't change what it does to folks."

Sniffles hesitated, then moved closer. "You're talking about her, aren't you?"

Rex didn't respond immediately. The image of Miss Whiskers, poised and confident even in defeat, lingered in his mind. She was a puzzle he'd never fully solved, a creature of contradictions who could make betrayal feel like a favor. She'd walked away from the wreckage with her head held high, and Rex had let her go—not because he trusted her, but because he knew she'd find a way to twist whatever justice he tried to deliver.

"She played me, Sniffles," Rex admitted finally, his voice quieter. "Used me to clean up her mess, and now she's out there, probably already weaving her next web."

Sniffles scratched the back of his neck. "Yeah, but you saw through it in the end. That's gotta count for something."

"Does it?" Rex turned to face him, his sharp gaze cutting through the dim light of the office. "I've been at this game long enough to know the difference between winning and surviving. This? This was surviving."

Sniffles didn't have an answer for that. He just nodded, his eyes downcast, and wandered over to the desk, where Rex's battered notebook lay open. He flipped through a few pages, the scribbled notes and half-finished thoughts a testament to the chaos of the case.

"What're you gonna do now?" Sniffles asked after a long pause.

Rex crushed his cigarette in the ashtray, his movements deliberate. "Same thing I always do. Wait for the next poor sap to walk through that door and hope they're not lying through their teeth."

Sniffles chuckled nervously. "Think you'll ever get a case that's not a mess?"

Rex smirked, pulling his hat low as he leaned back in his chair. "Not in this city, kid. But that's why they come to me. I don't clean up messes—I survive them."

The two sat in silence for a while, the distant hum of the city their only companion. Rex didn't know what the future held, but he knew Barkington would never stop throwing challenges his way. And he wouldn't stop meeting them, not until the city swallowed him whole.

For now, that was enough.

www.ingramcontent.com/pod-product-compliance
Lightning Source LLC
Chambersburg PA
CBHW021434150726
47989CB00001B/239